A Candlelight
Regency Special

The Unsuitable Lovers

Phoebe Matthews

A CANDLELIGHT REGENCY SPECIAL

Published by
Dell Publishing Co., Inc.
1 Dag Hammarskjold Plaza
New York, New York 10017

Dell ® TM 681510, Dell Publishing Co., Inc.

ISBN: 0-440-14953-3

Printed in the United States of America

First printing—October 1981

The Unsuitable Lovers

Amelia Grant stormed up the staircase, her slipper toes banging against the risers.

"Where is he?" she cried. "Where is he?" and the sound of doors clicking shut echoed about her.

They were all cowards, her sisters, cook, the daily, all slipping out of sight, closing doors, hurrying down hallways. Not that it mattered; it was not them she sought. She caught her father's bedchamber doorknob, threw the door open, and drew some consolation from its crash against the wall. Her father sat in his wide four-poster, his nightshirt tied at the ruffled neck, his nightcap slipped forward over his eyebrows. He peered at her, his watery eyes wide with innocence.

"Sir, you have done it again," Amelia exclaimed, and tossed a snowstorm of billings across his counterpane. A loosened ribbon slid from her hair and fluttered unnoticed to the floor.

"Amelia, my dear," he said softly.

"Don't you dare 'Amelia dear' me! How could you do this to me?"

"What is it that I have done?" he asked.

"What? Begging your indulgence, sir, let me ask this! Did you touch the money box? And if not you, then, pray tell, who did? Are you accusing cook? Are you accusing the daily? The yardman? Dare you accuse one of your own daughters?"

"No, no, my dear, of course I would not."

"Then who took the money from the box?" Amelia's face flushed beneath the shadow of her unruly mass of dark curls. Her large blue eyes glittered. She chewed her lower lip, unknowingly deepening the dimple at her mouth's left corner.

The old man slid down into his pillows until Amelia could see nothing of him but his face, a wrinkled pink ball in a cloud of white cap, ruffles, and tatting-edged bed linens. He whispered, "I suppose I must have done, my dear."

"Suppose? Father! You have a doubt then?"

"Amelia, my darling, it seemed such an opportunity. I only thought to win a bit to spend on luxuries for yourself and your sisters."

"I am sure you did," she scoffed. "Pray tell, how much did you win, sir?"

"I—I—uh—I did not actually—"

"You came home penniless, didn't you? You have done it again, spent every last shilling, and left me to face your creditors! Father, what is to become of us?"

Sinking onto the edge of his bed, Amelia sat staring away from him, her hands pressed to the top of her head. If she let them fall loose to her side, she seriously feared she would strike him, and as Berdine was forever reminding her, she was supposed to honor her parent.

He reached out a trembling hand and patted her arm. "There, my dear, it can't be that bad."

"It is worse than that bad," Amelia moaned. "We owe everyone. How long do you think the butcher will continue to carry us? And the roofer has threatened to turn your debt over to a solicitor. And cook? And the daily? And the yardman? Their wages are six months past due! I don't mind for myself, but Berdine and Clarisse are ashamed to go to Sunday service, their clothes are so shabby, and Daphne doesn't even know what a new gown is, she has worn made-overs for so many years. Are we all to end up in Newgate?"

"No one in my family has ever gone to debtors' prison," the old man said calmly, "so neither can we."

"Father, no one has ever gone to prison in your family because no one before you has taken every penny of his income and gambled it away. There is an end to our inheritance and we are rapidly approaching it. This house will be sold from over our heads to pay your debts. And where shall we live then?"

"I am sure we will live someplace," he said, and smiled at her. "I have always lived someplace."

Amelia shrieked, leapt to her feet, glanced at the old man, clenched her fists, and ran from the room. She clattered down the stairs, her muslin skirts billowing around her ankles, and marched down the hallway into the morning room.

Sunrays slanted over the mended table linen, the crosshatch pattern of light through the multipaned windows stretching across the thin carpet. The room was a jumble of mismatched furnishings, from Grandmother Grant's oak dresser with its square lines and dentil cornice fretting to Grandfather Stafford's heavy oval mahogany dining table on its cabriole legs to Third Cousin Augusta's discarded collection of flimsy, hooped-back chairs.

Her sisters sat over their breakfast cups, Berdine pouring tea, Clarisse pushing her sausage about her plate with her knife tip, and Daphne spreading her bread with the absolute last of the jam. Clarisse and Daphne looked almost alike except that Clarisse was four years older, and while Clarisse played with her food, eating almost nothing, Daphne consumed every crumb she could reach.

In the morning glow their two blond heads flamed gold, while their complexions shone rose-petal soft above the faded ruffles of their muslin dresses. It was the sort of setting that made the vicar's wife clasp her hands to her bosom and sigh, "Clarisse and Daphne look exactly like angels!"

"Are you quite done with shouting?" Berdine asked softly.

"I wouldn't mind his gambling if only he won," Amelia said.

"Amelia! Win or lose, gambling is a sin. I cannot see that it matters which way his fortune goes."

"It matters not at all if you are quite prepared to live out your life in Newgate."

Clarisse gasped and stared, open mouthed. Daphne bit into her bread, dribbling jam on her chin, and ignored Amelia.

Berdine sat motionless, a cup in one hand, the chipped blue ironstone teapot in the other. She reminded Amelia of a startled squirrel that had stopped in midaction, its eyes wide, its tiny nose and ears raised, alert yet statue-still. Berdine rather resembled a squirrel, except for her pearly skin tones, with her thick brown braid, her round face, her small features, and her plain gray gown trimmed only by a wide brown sash beneath her bosom. While the rest of them were tall and slim, Berdine was short and gently rounded. Undisciplined dimples peeked from her elbows and wrists, sometimes belying her pious expression.

"Has it come to that?" she asked.

"We might stall our creditors six months more but little else," Amelia said.

Clarisse asked, "Are we to be thrown out on the street?"

"No one would do that, dear," Berdine said.

"They would, indeed, dear," Amelia said. "Berdine, we must stop living in a dream. It is over. The money is gone. You must all listen to me. You also, Daphne."

"Daphne is only a baby," Berdine said.

"Fourteen is not a baby. Fourteen is old enough to share the burden," Amelia said. "I have known this day would come, though I had hoped not so soon, but as there is no choice left us, we must think seriously of what to do."

"We shall do whatever you suggest, Amelia dear. We always have," Berdine said.

Amelia choked back a sob of despair. For the past ten years, since her mother's death, she had run the household and raised her sisters, though she had been only twelve years of age at the start. Her father had always spent his inheritance lightly, buying whatever caught his fancy and stopping often with gaming friends, but his wife had kept him within bounds. After her death he lost any sense of responsibility and, more, Amelia feared, any real idea of the amounts of money he let slip away.

Mister Grant was like a child, yet he was still master of the house and Amelia could control him only through threats and wheedling, not by any legal means. If any of her sisters had possessed some ability to manage, that would have eased her burden, but all were as helpless as her father in money matters. Berdine could quote any Bible verse requested of her, Clarisse could tat endless lengths of trimming to sew on petticoats and bed linens, and Daphne was surprisingly quick at her French lessons, but none of them knew a penny from a shilling.

"I have one plan in mind," Amelia said, "but, Berdine, it would require much of you."

"With the Lord as my shepherd, I can do whatever is required of me," Berdine said.

"Yes, oh, as for that, I wish the Lord knew more about paying accounts," Amelia said.

Berdine closed her eyes in silent prayer. Berdine seldom criticized, but she prayed often. Amelia rather thought she would have preferred criticism.

"What do you plan?" Clarisse asked.

"Do you all remember Great-aunt Sophie?"

Berdine, eyes still closed, shuddered.

Amelia said quickly, "Yes, umm, her last visit was perhaps not too pleasant. She is perhaps a bit—uh—a bit outspoken. Still, she is the only relative we've got—"

Daphne interrupted, "Do you mean that funny old woman who came here four or five years ago and had that perfectly terrible row with father?"

"A bit outspoken," Amelia continued, "but she did say that she would present us to society if we ever wished to join her in Bath during the Season."

"Us to society!" Berdine's eyes flew open. "You

have lost your senses, Amelia! We have no clothes, to start with."

"I should much prefer a season in London," Clarisse said.

"Do you know anyone in London?" Amelia asked. Clarisse shook her head.

"Then, like her or not, Aunt Sophie is all we have, and with our situation what it is, I think we had best take advantage of her offer. She's none too young. When she dies, she will leave everything to her nephew. So if she is to help us, we must hurry."

"Dear," Berdine said, "we will do as you ask us, but what is it that you are asking?"

"I am asking us all to be practical and look at our situation in the glaring light of reason. The truth is this. None of us has any possibility of income at all. Our grandfather's will did not even leave settlements on us. We are quite on our own. And so far, I have not seen any suitors wearing out our doorstep."

"That is not true," Berdine said. "The vicar's brother is quite taken with you, Amelia. Why else would he call?"

"Oh, *me!*" Amelia exclaimed with a toss of her head. Her dark curls, free of their lost ribbon, slipped across her forehead, softening the annoyed expression on her pert face. She brushed the tendrils back with her restless hands. "Berdine, whatever may be the intentions of the vicar's brother, I have far too many responsibilities to consider marriage for myself. My only interest is to find husbands for the three of *you.*"

"Me?" Daphne said.

"Not yet, of course, but when you are older. Clarisse and Berdine are of good age now. And I do not intend that you should be wasted on any silly vicar's brother, either. Now listen, both of you, for this is my thinking. Berdine, for now you must remain here to care for Father and Daphne. I will write to Aunt Sophie and remind her of her offer. Then I shall take Clarisse for the Season and, with Aunt Sophie's help, I shall find a wealthy husband for Clarisse."

"I want more in a husband than wealth," Clarisse said.

"If you must choose between the poorhouse and wealth, wealth will suffice," Amelia said.

Clarisse pushed her sausage one more turn around her plate, her smooth brow furrowed with the effort of her thoughts. Slowly she asked, "Will I need party clothes?"

"You shall, indeed. Take Daphne with you and search the attic trunks. There must be something we can make over."

"But surely I will need something new—"

"Go and look!" Amelia shouted, and Clarisse and Daphne fled the morning room. She listened to them clatter up the stairs, past the bedrooms, and through the attic door.

"I am too old to be presented to society," Berdine said, but her voice wavered. "You are wise to take Clarisse. She is by far the prettiest of us."

"Twenty is hardly in your dotage," Amelia said. "And as for Clarisse, she isn't a bit prettier than you."

"The vicar's wife says that Clarisse looks like an angel."

"That's because the vicar's wife presumes that angels are blondes. I hear that brown hair and eyes are all the rage in London this year."

16

"Are they really?" Berdine asked, her small face puckered with doubt.

"Yes," Amelia lied, having no idea what the rage of London society might be, as she knew no one from London or its social crowd; but she did not want to cause Berdine sorrow. "I am taking Clarisse first because she is such a muttonhead, Berdine. I could not leave her here to manage, nor would I dare send her alone to Bath. Only the Lord could guess what she might pick for herself for a husband. I intend to go along and find her a proper gentleman. When she is cared for, I shall return here and you shall go to Bath."

"I don't think I would want to travel alone to Bath," Berdine complained, her dimpled hands twisting her skirt in agitation.

"I shall find a suitable abigail to travel with you," Amelia said. "And once there, dear, Aunt Sophie will take you into society and introduce you to suitable gentlemen. I am not worried about *you* choosing unwisely, Berdine."

Because, Amelia thought to herself, by that time I shall have made quite clear to Aunt Sophie the type of husband Berdine must have, and if I remember Aunt Sophie correctly, she will have no trouble guiding Berdine.

"Very well, Amelia. But once Clarisse and I are married, what will you do?"

Amelia tried to smile brightly to hide her fear. She had never actually seen Newgate, but she had heard of it often enough that in her imagination she could hear its doors clang shut behind her. "I am hopeful that if you and Clarisse both have rich husbands, one of you can provide a home for Daphne. If we can

17

accomplish this soon, I will have only Father to worry about. With but two of us, I can let cook and the daily go and send out the laundry, I should think, and cut our costs enough to repay our debts a bit at a time."

"I suppose if our husbands are rich, they might help with Father's debts," Berdine said.

"That would be heaven," Amelia sighed, "but I haven't much hope of gaining heaven that easily."

CHAPTER 2

Amelia poked her head out of the carriage window and stared up at the fawn-colored crescent of stone houses with their matching pillars and entries and windows. When the coachman opened the door, she dove into his arms in her eagerness to be out of the carriage, then bounded away to stand staring up at the tall building that ran all the way to the end of the cobbled street without a break, reflecting the winter sun back at her as though it were a sandstone cliff.

"The houses are all one!" she exclaimed. "They run right into each other! How can one know which house to enter?"

"By the number, miss," the coachman said.

"But—but—they have no side gardens! Look, Clarisse, have you ever! I can't believe it!"

Clarisse let the coachman lift her down, then stumbled sleepily to Amelia's side, making vague gestures with her gloved hands to smooth her traveling cloak and straighten her old fur-edged bonnet. The journey in the carriage that Aunt Sophie had sent to collect them at Pickerton Cross had been somewhat longer and far, far rougher than her expectations. She had never traveled further than the local market before this.

Amelia whirled about, soaking in the afternoon excitement of Bath. A vendor pulled a barrow piled high with carrots, leeks, and bunches of dried lavender. A delivery boy balanced on his head a basket filled with fragrant, steaming bread loaves. A fine carriage with six matched grays rounded the park that faced the crescent of solemn houses.

"You're letting the sun touch your complexion," Clarisse warned, but Amelia ignored her.

"The River Avon must be that way," Amelia said, pointing eastward. "Do you think it is too far to walk? I should like to see it."

From behind her a voice said, "Miss Grant? Miss Clarisse?"

Turning, Amelia saw that the coachman had already carried their one trunk to the door and, while a manservant shouldered it and disappeared within, a housemaid leaned out from the doorway, softly calling their names. She added, "Miss Stafford is waiting tea, miss."

Reluctantly, Amelia turned away from the crisp winter afternoon with its brilliant sky to enter the dark hallway. In the shadows pier glass mirrors glowed back the reflection of polished mahogany and crystal wall sconces.

"Would you like a wash, miss?" the maid said.

"Please, yes," Clarisse said quickly while Amelia gazed up the wide stairwell at the portraits in their dark-gold frames.

When the housemaid began to untie Amelia's bonnet ribbons, Amelia drew back, surprised. "Whatever are you doing?"

The maid blushed. "I'm sorry, miss. I meant to help."

Amelia, who had always considered herself capable of removing her outer garments by herself, not knowing that this was ever done any other way, smiled and said, "My thoughts were elsewhere. You startled me."

The girl set their bonnets and cloaks on a chair by the door, saying, "I'll brush them for you, miss. Come this way, if you will," and led them through a small parlor to a dressing room. On a marble-topped table stood a pitcher of warm water, a bowl of matching porcelain, and a set of brushes with ivory backs.

"Are these for us to use?" Clarisse asked.

"Yes, miss."

Clarisse and Amelia looked at each other and Amelia knew that her sister was thinking of their own warped washstand with its chipped ironstone bowl. She turned the brush in her hand. Not a wisp of hair or dust. The servant must clean it after every guest. What a tale she would have for the vicar's wife when she returned to Pickerton Cross. Amelia smoothed her traveling dress, frowning at her reflection in the mirror above the washbowl. She could see too clearly where the shoulder seams of her clothing had worn thin and showed a rust tinge against the dark-blue wool.

When the maid pulled open the double doors to the drawing room and announced their names, Amelia forgot the glories of the dressing room. Pale wood paneling, light brocaded draperies, tall French mirrors, and the most fragile and beautiful furnishings she had ever seen almost took away Amelia's breath.

From the center of a rose velvet settee a sharp

voice said, "These are my nieces, Richard. Do come in, my dears, and let me present my good friend, Sir Richard Wyland. Richard, their mother was a Stafford. She was my brother's daughter."

A tall, slim man who, had he been a portrait, would have been painted all in shades of warm golden-brown, unfolded himself from the edge of a needlepoint-covered chair and said, "You'd be Miss Grant and you are Miss Clarisse."

Clarisse turned her angel face up towards his, her mouth open.

He said, "You must be weary from your journey. Do come sit here, ladies," and although Amelia was unsure how he managed it, he seemed to guide them both to chairs, settle them gently with his fingers barely touching their elbows, and smile into both their faces. That, she supposed, was the way it was with the men who would be in Bath for the Season, displaying manners the likes of which one would not have seen in Pickerton Cross, even at the vicar's house.

As Clarisse had not yet closed her mouth or looked away from the gentleman's face, Amelia said quickly, "How kind it was of you to invite us to your home, Aunt Sophie. We have so looked forward to seeing you again. You're looking very well."

Amelia's great aunt overflowed the settee, not with her size but with her trimmings. She was a short, plump woman, dressed in rustling lavender silk with cascades of lace across the deep bodice, a sash at her waistline, and a wide skirt of many filmy layers. Her round face and the enormous halo of hair were heavily powdered, a practice that, like the dress, had been out of fashion for at least fifteen years. Yet the dress was obviously not old.

Aunt Sophie leaned forward and snapped, "I look my age and feel the same, Amelia. But you have changed." To Sir Richard she added, "It's been four years since I have seen my nieces. Clarisse was still a child."

Sir Richard leaned towards Clarisse and said, "And now she is a beautiful lady."

Clarisse continued to gaze at him, silent and slack-jawed.

"D'you think so?" Aunt Sophie asked. "They all look too thin to me, these modern girls. I can't imagine what they eat. Nothing, I suppose. Here, you had better have your tea before it goes cold, Amelia."

Amelia's hands trembled as she grasped the Rockingham cup and saucer, causing the thin silver spoon to rattle against the porcelain.

"There, you see, they eat so little they are all nerves. Have some cakes, Amelia, and try some of that pastry."

"Was the trip difficult, Miss Grant?" Sir Richard asked.

"I think not. I haven't traveled so much that I've anything to compare it to," she said, as she reached toward the tea table with its spellbinding array of gold-encrusted porcelain platters, covered with carefully arranged bits of breads and sweets. She had no idea what all the foods were. "We stopped at an inn for our midday meal. Do you live in Bath, Sir Richard?"

"My grandmother has a home here, Miss Grant. She comes for the waters."

"Is she ill, then?"

Aunt Sophie snorted, her round, powdered face creasing into an amused frown. "She is not ill, Amelia, she is old. Richard's grandmother is a dear friend of mine. We were girls together. And now we are all old. The waters of Bath will not make us young again, but they taste so vile that we delude ourselves that they will remove our aches."

"Would that my mind were as young and quick as yours, Miss Stafford," Sir Richard said.

She waved a jeweled hand at him. "Save your pretties for the foolish young women at the parties, Richard. They will be here soon enough. They begin to arrive now, Amelia, all the nieces and granddaughters and goddaughters, the wards, and the third, fourth, and fifth cousins, my dear, with their trunks of skimpy little frocks. If the frocks continue to shrink and the girls become any thinner, the gentlemen won't be able to find them at all."

Sir Richard said, "If you will pardon my saying it, my grandmother looks forward to the Season with great expectation, Miss Stafford, and so, I must suppose, do you. Especially now that you have two such lovely ladies to introduce."

"I am not complaining, Richard. If you young people did not come for the Season, Bath would have no residents except those of us who haven't quite got around to dying yet. The town would be as merry as a churchyard."

Amelia popped a sweet into her mouth, was startled by its unusual and slightly unpleasant flavor, and wondered what it was and what she would do if she could not manage to swallow it. If she had been alone with her aunt and sister, she would have raced into the hallway and spit the sweet into her hand, but as

Sir Richard sat between herself and the door, she tried instead to wash it down with the tea.

She swallowed too quickly. The food went down, but the tea touched that spot in her throat that made her gag. She clapped her hands over her mouth, her shoulders shaking.

"Miss Grant, are you ill?" she heard Sir Richard say, and felt his hand slap gently between her shoulder blades. He forced his large handkerchief to her face, adding, "Cough it out, don't choke to death!"

The blood flowed to her face, burning her cheeks, but not from choking. She coughed into his handkerchief, then sat still, her face buried in the soft cloud of linen and tatting, too embarrassed to look up at him.

Why had she ever thought she could bring her sisters here and present them to society when none of them knew anything of city manners, not even how to identify sweets on a tea tray? She sniffed in self-pity.

His hand remained gently on her back, its warmth penetrating her frock. "Are you better now, Miss Grant?"

She nodded.

"Perhaps you would care to lie down? Shall I call the maid to help you to your room?"

Amelia shook her head, her face still hidden in his handkerchief.

His hand moved away from her back. Where it had been, her skin still felt warm under the wool cloth. Slowly she lowered the handkerchief and took a deep breath, then looked in horror for the Rockingham cup, expecting to see it broken on the carpet. It sat before her on the tea table, complete with its saucer and spoon, and she realized he must have caught it from her shaking fingers when she first began to choke.

"I am so sorry, Aunt Sophie," she said.

"I should think you would be," her aunt sniffed. "I do believe you choked on my favorite gooseberry pastry. It is a specialty of mine; my cook is the only one in Bath who knows its secret. I guard the receipt as closely as I guard my jewels, Amelia."

Sir Richard settled back into his chair and smiled at Amelia. "Between us, I have never cared for gooseberry, either."

He had, Amelia decided at that moment, the nicest smile imaginable. It tilted the corners of his mouth and drew a fine line from jaw to brow that ended at the crinkled outer edges of his eyes. More still, it erased the stiff perfection of the drawing room and made her feel as though she were home in her own parlor.

She smiled back.

Aunt Sophie said, "It may amuse you to come to tea and insult my most treasured receipts, Richard, but you must repay me with a bit of gossip."

"What might I know that would be unknown to you, Miss Stafford?" His gaze drew slowly away from Amelia to her aunt.

"I hear that Lady Elspeth will arrive in time for the Chastletons' party. Tell me, pray, what brings her ladyship to Bath? Since when is our Season brilliant enough to attract the likes of her?"

The gentleman leaned back in his chair, looked solemnly at his lavender-and-powder hostess, and then chuckled softly. "Not much escapes your notice, my dear Miss Stafford."

"Nothing escapes my notice," Aunt Sophie retorted. "And what of your grandmother? What does she say?"

"Ah, then you think the arrival of her ladyship would be of interest to my grandmother?"

"Do you mean she doesn't yet know?"

Not knowing of whom they spoke, or why, Amelia let her mind wander to a study of the gentleman. He was pleasantly handsome, well mannered certainly, but what most caught her attention was his clothing, so different from the attire of the gentlemen of Pickerton Cross. Was this the latest fashion? No doubt she would soon learn. She appraised him from his silk cravat and striped vest to his pale breeches and gleaming boots, fascinated most by the narrow cut of his gold velvet coat. As her glance rose to his face, she met his eyes gazing back at her and realized they were all sitting in silence now.

"Is there something in my dress that disturbs you, Miss Grant?" he asked.

Amelia froze, horrified to be caught staring. She stuttered, "I—I—I have never seen—such a handsome coat, Sir Richard. It is quite—quite—"

"Quite ridiculous," Aunt Sophie exclaimed. "It really is, Richard. No wonder you leave the child speechless. Where have they gone, the elegant men of my youth? Ah, I remember all too well the way your grandfather looked when he courted me, embroidered edgings on his coat and lace edgings everywhere. One never sees a proper jabot now. Don't interrupt, Richard. It is true, you know, he did court me. My family was in London, you see, but I would have none of him."

27

"You were ever your own person, dear Miss Stafford."

"I had not yet met Mary Wollstonecraft, mind, no, that was many years later. She was much younger than I, but still, even before meeting her I had already thought on the ideas she was to expound. I had quite made up my mind to remain unwed."

"Then obviously my grandfather had no style at all," Sir Richard said, flashing a quick smile at Amelia. "Had he worn a coat as fine as mine, surely you would have accepted him."

Aunt Sophie laughed. "His coat was fine enough but he had not your quick tongue, boy. And that is just as well for you. Otherwise *I* might have been your grandmother."

Sir Richard held out a hand to Amelia and his other hand gestured towards Clarisse. "Dear Miss Stafford, by rejecting my grandfather, you have robbed me of the opportunity to be related to these lovely ladies. How bad of you."

He said more, but Amelia lost the direction of his words. His gesture reminded her that Clarisse was in the room and for the first time since their entry, she looked at her sister.

Clarisse still sat speechless, her wide gaze fastened on Sir Richard, her mouth slightly open. In her graceful hands she cradled a porcelain cup, the tea long since gone cold.

CHAPTER 3

When Aunt Sophie looked into their trunk, her only reaction was to drop the lid quickly and say to the housemaid, "Dora, send my modiste word that she must come here at once!"

Dora, a solid girl with high color and unruly taffy-colored hair, bobbed her understanding and scurried out of the room, a flash of striped poplin dress and flying apron ribbons.

"She'll do for a dresser, I suppose," Aunt Sophie sighed, and sank into a tapestry-covered chair by the balcony window.

"We don't need anyone to dress us, Aunt Sophie," Amelia said.

"My dear, of course you do. It may be all very well to attire oneself in Pickerton Cross, but in Bath, no. And as for the attire itself, my modiste, Mrs. Lake, is quite clever. She will know what you must wear for each occasion."

"Are we to have new dresses, then?" Clarisse asked.

"Perhaps your—your modiste will be able to make over some of our gowns to meet the style," Amelia said.

"Make over? Why should she do that? No," Aunt

Sophie insisted, "if you are to be outfitted, let it be proper."

"But the cost—"

"Dear Amelia, in this world there are only two things worth inheriting, money and title. As my father was a mere baronet, he could give me no title, a point I deeply regretted as a young woman. Now that I am older and much wiser, I am eternally grateful that he was a rich baronet rather than a poor duke. How pleasant it is to be wealthy Miss Stafford rather than penniless Lady Sophie."

"Yes, but—"

"And being wealthy, I may have my own way. Not another word, Amelia. I shall no doubt despise the gowns Mrs. Lake makes for you, but I shall have the comfort of knowing that all Bath society will acknowledge the quality of my nieces' attire."

And so it was that Amelia and Clarisse found themselves standing motionless in their thin, mended petticoats for endless hours while Mrs. Lake, her mouth filled with pins, draped yards of cambric and velvet and silk around them. She would even have to make new petticoats, she warned, as theirs were much too full, and when she returned the next day with their first garments, Amelia's shock almost matched Aunt Sophie's.

Her undergarment was no more than a fragile slip of lace and silk that clung to her body. When Mrs. Lake pulled the gown over her head and worked it into place, Amelia longed to dive back into the security of her wool traveling dress.

"I might wear this to bed," Amelia protested, "but I do not care to leave my chamber in it."

"Oh, it is so beautiful!" Clarisse cried, clapping her hands together.

Aunt Sophie said, "Mrs. Lake, are you quite sure this is what the young ladies are wearing this season?"

"Yes, madam, indeed, as you see, I have left in the sleeves. In London the dresses are far more revealing."

"Must save all sorts of expense on cloth," Aunt Sophie snorted.

Amelia was dragged to the mirror by her sister. Slowly she lowered her gaze from her neck to hemline. The summer blue of the cambric brought out the color of her eyes. That, she thought, was all that could be said for the gown. It left her throat exposed to winter winds and anyone's stares, with barely enough cloth to enclose her bosom. The high silk sash held her ribs to very shallow breathing. The narrow skirt clung to her hips, outlined her lower limbs, and stopped well above her slippers.

"It is perfection," Mrs. Lake said, "because, my dear Miss Grant, you have the perfect figure. You will be the envy of every young lady in Bath and the object of devotion of every gentleman."

Amelia could see that this might be so for Clarisse and said slowly, "Mrs. Lake, you may dress my sister thus. For myself, I shall keep this dress because it is done, but my other gowns must be of heavier material, higher at the throat and a bit longer."

"But, my dear—"

"No, I must explain to you, Mrs. Lake, I am two and twenty, well past girlhood, and have come to Bath as chaperone to my sister. I do not wish to appear as anything other than part of the background at parties."

"Oh, I see, Miss Grant. But of course, I will cut your gowns as you wish, though it does seem a shame."

"I want my gowns cut *exactly* like that," Clarisse cried, pointing to Amelia's new dress. "And you need not make the sleeves to my wrist."

"Indeed, no, I shall do some short sleeves for you, Miss Clarisse."

"Tell me," Amelia said dryly, "how many young ladies take to their beds with fever by the Season's end?"

After Mrs. Lake had left them and Dora had folded away their new gowns, Amelia and Clarisse sank into deep chairs and gazed out the tall windows to the winter garden, where the snow drifted like powder through the dark, gnarled branches of the thorn trees and melted when it touched the pebble paths. Amelia drew her ruffled wrapper closely around herself until the rows of tatting tickled her chin.

"I can't think why you wish to hide away," Clarisse said. "If you didn't say it, no one would know your age."

"We are not here to find a husband for me, Clarisse. Indeed, I want you to wear the prettiest gowns possible and be the envy of everyone. For myself, I should prefer to sit out the dances or perhaps join Aunt Sophie in whist."

"I should like to dance every dance with that handsome Sir Richard Wyland," Clarisse said.

Closing her eyes, Amelia tried to imagine herself at a ball, dressed in satin, caught in Sir Richard's firm grasp, smiling into his eyes. She could not. He had been pleasant enough over the tea tray, but at a ball he would hardly notice her. In her mind he drifted away, whirling some other lady onto the floor, chatting in clever phrases about the latest Bath gossip, while she remained at Aunt Sophie's side. Indeed, that was as she had intended when she came to Bath. In her dark simple clothing, from the shadows of an inconspicuous corner, she would watch for a suitable gentleman for Clarisse, all the time listening to the talk of aunts and grandmothers to better learn each gentleman's qualifications. A flirtation for herself might be a pleasant memory to take back from Bath, but it would divert her attention from her purpose and she could not afford to waste the time. Even now she worried as to how Berdine was managing the household and putting off the creditors.

Their first ball was not a ball, Aunt Sophie insisted, only a small party at the home of her dear friend, the Countess of Alderwood, Sir Richard's grandmother. The old earl, disliking any form of entertainment that required him to dress, never came to Bath but remained, instead, at his estate where, Lady Alderwood explained to Amelia, he could muck about with his precious pigs. *She* preferred the cobbled streets, the Assemblies, the opera, and the many other advantages of Bath, including the waters.

Amelia nodded, but her attention wandered around Lady Alderwood's magnificent ballroom. Its ceiling met in high arches above carved pillars that reflected the prism crystals of the many chandeliers. Fragile satinwood chairs lined the walls. The musicians played on a raised stage backed by velvet draperies. The polished floor shone beneath the swirling rainbow of beautifully gowned and jeweled ladies and elegant gentlemen. If this was a small party, Amelia did not think her heart could withstand the onslaught of a full-blown ball.

"I give these little gatherings in hopes that my grandson will be tempted to remarry, but I invariably fail, my dear," the countess confided. "He comes to act the host for me out of a sense of duty. Richard was ever mindful of his duty, even as a lad, which of course is why he was knighted, but now that he has married and produced a male heir for his estate, he sees no reason to remarry."

"Perhaps he is still mourning his wife's loss," Amelia said, trying not to show her surprise that Aunt Sophie had not told her Sir Richard was a widower.

"Tish! That was eight years ago when the boy was born and they'd only been married the one year. Not that I mean to dismiss his wife, my dear. She was a sweet enough little thing, though I found her dull, but it was not a love match. No, I know my grandson. He prefers his freedom. Oh, he takes the management of his estate seriously enough—in that he's rather like my husband—but all else is frippery with him."

"I cannot imagine him mucking about with the pigs," Amelia exclaimed, then raised her hand to her mouth as though she might push the words back down her throat. "Oh, I do apologize, Lady Alderwood."

The countess's watery eyes peered out from the wrinkled mask of her thin, heavily powdered face. Without the trace of a smile she said, "No need to apologize. Let me correct your flattering supposition

Unfortunately, my dear, all the men in my family are pig-muckers."

"Oh, I say, that's putting rather a point on it, madam," a voice said.

Amelia looked up into Sir Richard's face.

"Richard, my darling," the countess cried, "there you are! And would you have me mislead this lovely child?"

He bent over his grandmother and touched his lips to her brow. If he had seemed beautifully attired at their first meeting, he was quite beyond Amelia's ability to describe now. How could she ever tell the vicar's wife that a gentleman of Bath wore a cut velvet coat fit for the Regent, with twistings of cream silk at his throat and wrist and a vest that drew the eye, despite one's efforts at discretion, to his narrow waist? And—she quickly raised her eyes—the frame of hair around his laughing face shone the same gold-brown as satinwood.

"My dear Miss Grant," he said, "Why are you hidden away from view with the grandmothers? I saw your sister on the floor."

"I prefer to sit out," Amelia said, as she had said to at least three earlier gentlemen—but none of them had been so tempting.

"Then let me beg you to stand up with me. You cannot refuse your host."

"What sort of host are you, Richard, to appear an hour late?" the countess demanded.

"My darling, I do apologize, but I was detained."

The countess ran her fingers across her heavy diamond necklace as though checking to be sure none of the stones was missing. Tilting her head toward Amelia, she let one eyelid droop. Amelia could not believe it was a wink. No, the countess's eyelids drooped with age, surely, and not with purpose. The countess said flatly, "Detained, no doubt, with pig-mucking."

"What is this talk of pigs?" Sir Richard demanded. "Miss Grant, do not leave me to stand here bent over in this difficult position. Come stand up with me and let me converse on more suitable subjects."

"Are you questioning my choice of subjects?" the countess asked.

"Madam! Never! But surely you will allow me to steal Miss Grant away before the musicians give up entirely."

"I am sorry," Amelia said. "Truly, sir, I do intend to sit out. As I have refused other gentlemen, I do not believe I can accept you now."

"Nonsense, other gentlemen are not your host. Come along, dear lady," he said, and all but pulled her from her chair, so firmly did he catch her hand and draw her after him.

"Really, Richard," his grandmother scolded, "a gentleman waits for a lady to accept."

He caught Amelia in a light grasp and whirled her across the floor, beyond sight and hearing of his grandmother, whispering almost in her ear, "Ah, she is still trying to instruct me in me manners, gel."

Amelia could not suppress a giggle. "Truly, Sir Richard, I can believe you are a trial to the countess."

"Is my behavior so poor, then?"

"Oh, what would I, a simple 'gel' from Pickerton Cross, know of society's behavior, sir?"

"I think you are having fun with me," Sir Richard said, holding her at arm's length and peering into her face. "Would you play with words, miss? Indeed, I see you think you can belittle a poor pig farmer."

"What is this talk of pigs?" Amelia asked.

"Ah, there you have my family's deepest secrets. Understand swine, dear lady, and you understand the Wylands. The earl boasts the finest, largest, most productive sow this side of London. If I told you the size of her litters, you would blush. Are you versed in pigs, Miss Grant?"

"No—that is, I have never lived in the country. I am afraid my only acquaintance with animals is a lap dog and the kitchen cats."

"Then you do not ride?"

"I fear not. Will that completely destroy my social position in Bath, sir?"

He laughed and pulled her what seemed a bit close for a country dance, but as she glanced past his shoulder she noticed that the men of Bath did, indeed, hold the ladies in somewhat more intimate relationships than did the gentlemen of Pickerton Cross. Before Amelia had time to consider whether or not she enjoyed the nearness of her partner, her glance fell on Clarisse dancing by, held at arm's length by a pleasant-looking young man. His otherwise even features were drawn into lines of strain and he seemed to be talking intently, indeed, even nervously and quickly. Clarisse, from the back, was all soft golden curls, shimmering pink gown, and pale, graceful arms, but when her partner swung her about, Amelia stared directly into Clarisse's face and found her eyes wide, her full mouth hanging slack as though she were the village idiot.

"Do you not think so?" the young man's voice said, then anxiously filled the silence following his question with "But then, perhaps you have not considered it. Let me ask you another way, madam. Have you ever tried the new waltz step?" Again silence, then his quick reply, "Myself, I find it quite intriguing—"

Amelia longed to reach over and pinch Clarisse, but she and her partner had whirled out of reach.

"Did your aunt pick your lovely dress?" Sir Richard asked.

"No, I chose the color and style. Her modiste, a Mrs. Lake, made it for me. Do you like it, then?"

"I like the lady who wears it. The color seems a trifle somber."

Tilting back her head to better look at him, Amelia laughed. She knew quite well what he was thinking of her in her long-sleeved, high-throated dark-blue dress, with only its pale-green sash as a concession to Mrs. Lake's dismayed cries. "With a black sash, I could possibly use it for mourning," she said.

"You do not in any way look like an abigail," Sir Richard admitted, "but the dress, were it in a poorer fabric, would suit. Clever of you, you know. The room overflows with flower colors. You've turned every gentleman's head, wondering who is the lady in the unusual dress, and once turned, they've seen what a beauty you are and shall trample me to reach you."

"I hope not!" Amelia exclaimed. "That was not at all my intention, truly. I wished to remain unnoticed and would not have danced at all had you not insisted."

"What a strange young woman you are, Miss Grant," he said. "Or—I have it!—you have come to Bath to accompany your sister but you yourself are already spoken for by some very fortunate young man in Pickerton Cross."

"That is only partly right," Amelia admitted.

"Would you care to tell me which part?"

She said, "Only if you will tell me the number of piglets, sir."

"Piglets?"

"You said your grandfather's prize sow had such a number of piglets in one litter that it would make me blush to hear, but you overestimate my ability to blush."

The music stopped before he could answer. Tucking her hand through his elbow, Sir Richard led her slowly toward the edge of the dance floor, murmuring close to her ear, "Sweet Miss Grant, if there is truly a young man in Pickerton Cross, I prefer not to hear of the muttonhead. Had he any sense, he would have kept you well in sight at all times."

Other couples moved by them, the men stiff backed, smooth shaven, and dressed in dark russets, pale champagne tones, and rich claret velvet, the women supple as flower stalks, their curls piled high and caught in ribbons or jeweled clips, their pale gowns clinging to their graceful forms. Their elders sat in clusters of lavender and gray, watching, noting, comparing. Through an archway Amelia could see a more brightly lit room, its cream brocade draperies drawn closed against the night, circling the whist tables. If the dance floor, with its youthful crowd, resembled a spring garden, the gaming room flickered like a winter's evening, the candlelight and fireglow flashing on the heavy diamond ornaments covering wrists, fingers, throats, and twined through the powdered masses of white hair. Even the gentlemen's heads were snowcapped.

"If you have quite finished with hiding the lady away from the rest of us," a soft, masculine voice said, "do me the kindness of an introduction, Sir Richard."

"Ah, Miss Grant, I am forced to present the Viscount Pendarvin," Sir Richard said.

The viscount caught Amelia's hand, lifted it to his lips, and took her so by surprise that it wasn't until she stared down at the back of his head with its thick mass of waves that she realized what he was doing. And just in time. She had almost jerked away her hand.

He raised his face to smile shyly at her, then straightened. His eyes were as dark as his hair, his features as classic as a statue's, and his voice, had she been younger and more foolish, would have reminded her of girlhood dreams.

As it was, Amelia fluttered her eyelashes nervously.

Pendarvin was young, no older than Berdine, Amelia guessed. He asked, "Are you Miss Stafford's niece?"

"Yes, my lord."

"I do tremendously admire Miss Stafford. When she was young, she was famous for her stamina on walking trips," he exclaimed, and then, to Amelia's surprise, a blush of color spread across his face. "That is, my mother—my mother tells me so."

"I shall tell my aunt," Amelia said.

"Oh! I—she wouldn't be put out?"

"She'll think it quite a compliment," Amelia said,

vaguely remembering some mention of walking tours in connection with her great-aunt's youth.

Lord Pendarvin stared at her as though he wished to say something more, and Amelia waited, at once sympathetic. Something in his young confusion reminded her of Clarisse.

"Could—ah—that is—"

"Speak out, Charles, and then say your farewells," Sir Richard said. His light eyes twinkled with amusement but Amelia thought his remark unkind.

She said, "Yes, my lord?"

"Could—oh, would—would Miss Stafford welcome me if I should—should come to call?"

"Not likely," Sir Richard said.

"I cannot think why not," Amelia said.

"And you, Miss Grant? Would you be there if I called?"

"I am staying with my aunt. Yes, I would be there, as would my sister Clarisse."

"Clarisse? Oh! The lady with the golden hair!" A confused frown troubled his brow. He smiled quickly, adding softly, "Yes, I have met your sister. I have had the pleasure of her company in a set, you see. But what of you, Miss Grant? Is your program filled?"

Shaking her head, Amelia said, "My host has insisted on his right to one dance, but I did not come tonight to dance and would prefer to sit out."

"It is of no use to argue, Charles," Sir Richard said. "The lady has a firm mind."

Pendarvin's face relaxed in such obvious relief that Amelia bowed her head to hide her smile. He said, "But that is splendid, Miss Grant. That is, I mean, dancing exhausts me, as I have no grace at it. I should much prefer—thing is—ah, could I have the pleasure of keeping you company on the sidelines?"

Sir Richard leaned forward and whispered into Amelia's hair, "Beware, Miss Amelia Grant, of lords who pretend they cannot dance." Straightening, he added, "If you will accept such company as His Lordship, I must excuse myself to perform my required hostly duties."

CHAPTER 4

Amelia watched Sir Richard disappear into the crowd, then let the young viscount guide her to a chair. He said, "The Wylands have always taken duty seriously, be it to guest or country."

"Yes, my lord, so someone else said to me. Perhaps it was Lady Alderwood."

"She would, of course. I mean, after all, he is her grandson."

"Oh, do you think she would be prejudiced?" Amelia asked, careful not to smile.

"I would never argue with Lady Alderwood, madam. A man would be a real nimbrain to do that. Still, like my mother says, every diamond has its flaw."

Amelia peered closely into his face to see if he were jesting, saw all too well that he was not, and said, "I am sure your mother is correct."

"She usually is," he admitted, but did not sound overly happy.

"She—ah—your mother—is she interested in walking tours? You mentioned that she spoke of my aunt's past accomplishments."

"No, it's me," he said. "Thing is, I'm quite tied up

in them, planned to be on one now, except my mother put up a row about me attending this do."

"Then you find parties so very dull?"

"Oh, no! That is, I didn't mean—it's that I don't put much by dancing, seems a silly thing—but so does all the primping—I feel like a fool dandy," he said.

His clothing was of flawless taste, beautifully made, but Amelia noticed now that his neckcloth was awry, his collar wrinkled, and his cuffs bunched unevenly, as though someone had dressed him properly and then sent him off to the party. And he, like a small boy, had managed to disarrange his attire on the way.

"Tell me," Amelia said, "what was your impression of my sister?"

"Your sister? Oh, Miss Clarisse! A real stunner!"

Amelia's glance swept the room until she found Clarisse. Hiding her dismay at what she saw, she asked, "And what did you two converse about, my lord?"

She felt, rather than heard, his embarrassment, the slight twisting of his throat inside his neckcloth, the hesitation in his answer. At last he said, "Oh, this and that."

So she had not said one word to him, either, Amelia knew, as she watched her sister whirl by on the arm of another chattering, nervous young man, Clarisse's face a blank, her eyes wide and staring, her mouth hanging open.

Although Clarisse's program had been filled almost before she moved from the entry up the wide staircase to the ballroom, and she danced every dance, Amelia knew by the evening's end that she should withdraw Clarisse from Bath society immediately. Yet she lacked the heart to do so. Clarisse returned from the party glowing, and sat awake long after Dora had helped her into her nightgown and herself had gone to bed.

Clarisse bent over her program, squinting in the candlelight, reading aloud the names of the gentlemen who had been her partners.

"I could dance forever," Clarisse exclaimed. "Have you ever seen so many handsome gentlemen?"

Amelia said, "Then you enjoyed yourself?"

"Oh, Amelia!" Clarisse sighed, clasping her hands to her heart.

"And what did you say to the gentlemen?" Amelia persisted.

"Say?"

"Yes, didn't they converse?"

Clarisse drew her brows into a frown, thinking. "Yes, I am sure they did. They all did. They told me where they lived and how they liked my gown, oh, things like that."

"And you. What did you say?"

"Me?" Clarisse looked up, wide eyed. "What would I say?"

"Clarisse, when someone speaks to you, you must speak in return."

"Must I?"

"But—but Clarisse! You have been to church parties in Pickerton Cross. You spoke to the young men there."

Clarisse thought about that, then said slowly, "But I know the boys of Pickerton Cross. I did not know the gentlemen at the dance tonight. Of what could I speak?"

Amelia said, "My dear, that's what people do at parties. They converse. You must remember to converse. Speak of the weather or the party decorations, but speak of something."

"The weather? Or decorations? Yes, I suppose I could," Clarisse said, and returned to her study of her program, squinting through the shadows.

Amelia lay awake that night thinking through her problem, sure that it was her own fault that she had not properly trained Clarisse in the art of conversation. Yet there was truth to what Clarisse said. In Pickerton Cross everyone knew everyone, and often had for generations, so that one could always find something to say.

Very well, she would have to begin now, although it was a bit late, to correct the lack of instruction to Clarisse. In the morning she would practice a few simple conversations with her, Amelia herself taking the part of the gentleman.

Now that she had thought of it, though, she could not keep her mind on her plan because, for reasons that she could not fathom, her mind kept drifting to her easy conversation with Sir Richard, to his tall, slim form, his shining hair, his almost insolent smile. She tried to force his image from her mind, but as she drifted into half-sleep, she felt his nearness as intensely as she had when he'd whispered into her ear some warning about lords who didn't dance.

Amelia spent the next morning, while her aunt slept, confined to her room with Clarisse. She had Dora bring up a breakfast tray, although Clarisse would have preferred to eat downstairs.

"We shall need the privacy," Amelia said after Dora had withdrawn. "Now, dear, I shall pour your tea and you shall pretend I am Aunt Sophie. What do you say as I hand you your cup?"

"Thank you, Aunt Sophie?"

"Good. Now, dear, do you take sugar? Lemon? Milk?"

"You know I take sugar, Amelia."

"No, no. I am still Aunt Sophie."

Clarisse giggled. "Not unless you stick your head in the powder box."

"Please, Clarisse, this is serious."

"Oh, then, yes, please, Aunt Sophie. I would like sugar."

"Good," Amelia said. "Now pretend I am a gentleman."

"A gentleman? What gentleman?"

"What—oh, pretend I am Sir Richard."

Clarisse giggled again.

"Are you enjoying your stay in Bath, Miss Clarisse?" Amelia said, lowering her voice.

Clarisse said, "Yes."

Amelia said, "Clarisse, surely you can say more than one word."

"Yes, Sir Richard," Clarisse said.

Amelia sighed. "More, Clarisse."

"What more is there to say?" Clarisse pouted.

"Surely there must be something you especially enjoy about your stay. Think of it and say it."

"Oh!" Clarisse thought, then said, "Yes, Sir Richard, the weather is very nice and I like the decorations."

Amelia sighed. She had not taught Clarisse to tat in one day, she recalled. In fact it had taken twice the time to teach. Clarisse that it had taken to teach Berdine or Daphne. But once Clarisse had mastered tatting, she had tatted and tatted and tatted. Every piece of clothing and every bit of linen in their household was trimmed with Clarisse's tatting. Perhaps it would be the same with conversation. Once she had managed to remember to try to converse, perhaps she would become the belle of banter.

When the young viscount came to call that afternoon, Amelia saw a small glimmering of hope. Aunt Sophie served tea, the viscount and Amelia chatted, and halfway through his visit Clarisse closed her slack mouth. Amelia nodded her encouragement. As Pendarvin stood and moved toward the door, Clarisse leaned forward and said clearly, "I do enjoy the weather today, my lord."

Pendarvin paused, his perfect features frozen in true statue stillness above his slightly wrinkled collar, then said softly, "Indeed, yes, Miss Clarisse."

Then he rushed out the door that the servant held open for him, completely forgetting to bow his farewell to his hostess.

When he was safely out of hearing, Aunt Sophie burst into a fit of laughter. "Young Charles is as handsome as a young stallion and has a similar portion of wits!"

Amelia was too mortified to speak. She had set such high goals for Clarisse. Was that her sister's fault? She had raised Clarisse. Certainly she could only blame herself that she had taught the girl to read and sew and to give orders to tradesmen but had never taught her how to visit with a gentleman. On the other side, when she was educating her sisters, it had not occurred to Amelia that she would one day hope to marry them to wealthy husbands. Perhaps that was the sort of planning that came naturally to a mother's mind, but she was not a mother. The thought had not occurred to her until monetary matters had forced her to consider carefully what the future might hold for her younger sisters.

"Did I forget and leave my mouth open?" Clarisse asked.

"No, dear," Amelia said. To her great-aunt she added, "Perhaps it would be wisest for us to return to Pickerton Cross."

"Pickerton Cross!" Aunt Sophie exclaimed. "I should think not! No, give it time, Amelia. You will see. She only needs a bit of practice. And as for that, so does Charles."

"Lord Pendarvin?"

"My dear, he tries his mother sorely. He's all of twenty and as handsome as a story prince, yet he won't go to London at all. Indeed, his mother is forced to pretend a wretched cough as an excuse to insist that he accompany her to Bath for treatment."

"I'm quite outside," Amelia exclaimed.

"It is simple enough to understand when you know that Charles is an only son. If he won't go to social functions, how is he to find a suitable wife? He spends all his time tramping the woods or taking walking tours. The only females he might meet that way would hardly be suitable mothers for a Pendarvin heir."

"Oh! Yes, that is a problem; still, if he's but twenty, surely there is no press."

Aunt Sophie leaned forward, lowered her voice, and said, "He was a late child, Amelia, born almost past the time of decency. His father was a childless widower and his mother was the second wife. They'd been married ten years, well past hope, when Charles arrived. They would not care to die without the comfortable knowledge of a grandchild."

Amelia chewed her lip thoughtfully, then asked, "Would they consider Clarisse a suitable wife for their son, considering that we haven't a farthing?"

Aunt Sophie snorted. "Money is the one thing they have. Clarisse is healthy and beautiful and of good family. They would be overjoyed."

"Then I hope she can learn to converse with His Lordship beyond commenting on the weather," Amelia sighed.

Amelia and Clarisse remained in Bath during the following weeks of countless parties and entertained a flow of gentlemen callers. Each visit showed some small improvement in Clarisse's ability to handle conversation. Very, very small.

With the dark, handsome young viscount Clarisse managed to state her view of the weather upon his arrival rather than at his departure, though she could say no more to him after that one statement. And although her eyes never left his face, she did hold her mouth closed in a frozen smile.

Pendarvin, in return, had little to say, so that Amelia and Aunt Sophie were forced to carry the conversation.

Young gentlemen without titles fared somewhat better. Mr. Percy vanDelwick, who, according to Aunt Sophie, was as rich as a nabob, had a very ordinary countenance and could, had it not been for his stylish dress, have been a neighbor in Pickerton Cross by looks. Clarisse showed considerable progress when she was able to sit in the same room with him without staring.

"I am delighted to see you again, Miss Clarisse," he gushed, as soon as Aunt Sophie had handed him his tea.

Clarisse thought a moment, then asked, "Have we met before?"

Amelia said quickly, "Mr. vanDelwick, my sister mentioned to me last night when we returned home from the party how much she enjoyed your company at supper."

Clarisse said, "Oh! That's right. You took me down to supper last night."

"It was my pleasure and honor," the young man said, gazing at Clarisse.

She felt his look, glanced at Amelia, waited, then seemed to realize that she must speak next. Carefully, Clarisse said, "The decorations at the party were nice."

Exhausted with that effort she turned her concentration on her teacup, stirring slowly while the tea turned cold and not looking up again until he had said his good-byes and left.

As the door closed, Aunt Sophie patted Amelia's hand and said, "He wouldn't do, anyway, my dear. Poor blood, you know, weak infants, and that sort of thing. I shouldn't care to see it mingled with the Stafford line."

"The chance of anyone mingling with the Stafford line appears remote," Amelia said, reviewing in her memory the long list of gentlemen who had made up Clarisse's dance partners over the past weeks. She would never have guessed that there were so many gentlemen in Bath. Somehow Clarisse had managed to acquire a new partner for each dance or situation, attracted to her as they were by her angelic looks, but none ever asked twice. That some came calling, Amelia had at first found encouraging, but as they generally made no more than the weakest attempt to engage Clarisse in conversation, she found her suspicions growing.

Miss Sophie Stafford, for all her lack of a title, had considerable social standing. To be in her good graces put one in the good graces of many another and important leader of Bath society. Perhaps it was not so strange that the young men used the presence of nieces in the house as an excuse to call. That they also spent much effort in exchanging pleasantries with Amelia impressed Amelia not at all. They could hardly do less, as she was Miss Stafford's guest. She returned their efforts in conversation, hoping to cover the lapse in her sister's wit, but kept her remarks remote enough to discourage any personal interest.

Once, when they were alone, Aunt Sophie had said, "I do think, Amelia, that we are promoting the wrong young lady. Given any encouragement, I do believe half the men of Bath would offer for you."

"Nonsense," Amelia said. "I am beyond the age of flirtations. And even if I were not and the gentlemen did regard me seriously, who would offer for me knowing that the package must include three young sisters and a debt-ridden father?"

"Perhaps if his debts were paid—" Aunt Sophie said.

"No, it would be of no use, Aunt Sophie. He has lost contact with the real world. In debt or out, he would simply return to the gaming tables and reverse whatever fortune might bring him."

"But what are you to do, my dear?"

"I must try to find satisfactory lives for my sisters beyond our household, then remain in it to exert what control I can over my father. Left to himself, he could gamble the fortunes of the Regent into bankruptcy."

"Then we must press on in our efforts," Aunt Sophie said, patting her powdered mop of hair back from its cascading descent over her forehead. Her jeweled fingers flashed. "With the official Season opening next week, I see that we must sit Clarisse down and teach her by recitation at least three other suitable conversational gambits beyond weather and decoration."

But as fate decreed, they had not the time. The very next morning's post brought Berdine's letter.

"Dearest Amelia," Berdine wrote, "The worst has befallen despite all my attempts to delay, though I fear I do not truly have any ability to control such events. You, dear Amelia, would no doubt have fared better, and I sorely regret that I have been unable to live up to your expectations of me. Father cannot or will not answer any of my queries, but the insistence of his creditors can hardly be ignored. The house is to be put up for sale, though I do not understand how or why, only when, and we must all be out of it within a fortnight. Do forgive me for managing so badly, Amelia, and do, please, tell me how I am to proceed."

"That's all?" Aunt Sophie asked, when Amelia

had read aloud the letter.

But it was not all. The next day's post brought another message.

"Amelia, dearest," Berdine wrote, "worse moves to worst! I do fear I pressed Father too far with my inquiries, and when I enlisted the vicar's help, which seemed right for me to do, he flew into quite a rage, threw all of his clothing that would fit into his portmanteau, and left on the stagecoach. Amelia, I do not know where he has gone! Now, I do not mean to disturb your calm or cause you undue concern, dear, but cook and the gardener have disappeared, too, because, I think, their wages were somewhat in arrears. The daily comes in twice a week, but otherwise Daphne and myself find ourselves alone. Not that you need worry, dear, for the vicar's wife has been most kind and calls regularly, as she has done since you left, and called again today, so I suppose I shall manage somehow, but I should like some advice as to whether you think I should begin to pack the porcelain."

This time Aunt Sophie did not ask if the letter contained more information, deciding that she had heard enough. Tightening her small mouth in her round, powdery face, she leaned toward Amelia and said firmly, "I see nothing for it but to send the carriage at once for Daphne and Berdine."

"It would be such an imposition," Amelia said weakly.

"Would you leave them there alone, then?" Aunt Sophie snapped. "Ridiculous, Amelia. If you are fortunate, you will hear no more from your foolish father, but in the between time, your sisters must come to me, though I hardly thought to adopt four full-grown girls at my age."

"And so you shall not," Amelia said. She stood straight, her small chin held proudly high. What she had let happen to her mind, she truly could not remember, but she realized that she had allowed herself to drift in a dream existence of parties and new frocks and useless chatter while her world fell apart. Ever before she had been the sensible one, the one who held together the Grant household, and now, though there might be no house, she was still responsible for the family.

"We must stop this charade," Amelia said. "I must find some sort of a living for myself and my sisters. Perhaps we could find some small, suitable quarters to rent and then I see no reason why we cannot support ourselves with our sewing. Surely others have done it before us."

"Tish," Aunt Sophie said. "I thought you had more sense than that, girl. The poorhouse overflows with seamstresses."

Amelia frowned, thinking. "We cannot remain here, Aunt Sophie, living in your debt. We are certainly not your responsibility and, although I appreciate your generosity—"

"You may be right," Aunt Sophie said, holding up a plump hand to stop Amelia. "You may, indeed. I do not object to you earning your own livelihood, Amelia. Indeed, I admire your courage. But I should like a more practical choice. I know that you are well read, but tell me of Berdine and Daphne. Have they Clarisse's wits?"

"Oh, no," Amelia exclaimed. "Berdine can quote

the Bible from memory and both read well and speak reasonable French."

"French? Your sisters speak French?"

"Indeed, madam, I did once think that if they should need it, it would allow them to accept positions as governesses, though that is not a fate I wish on them."

"Clever, girl, clever. But there you have it!"

"I do not see, Aunt Sophie, how that may aid us. Although Berdine and I could accept positions, Clarisse has only her sewing skills and Daphne is but fourteen."

Aunt Sophie leaned forward from her settee and rapped her fingernails on the edge of the tea tray to emphasize her point. Her rose lace skirts billowed about her.

"Amelia," she said, "as I have told you, many years ago I knew Mary Wollstonecraft. Not well, I regret, but I did meet her and have retained the highest admiration. She, you must know, had also to support herself, though I do believe her father was a drunkard or worse, but still, she had in her care sisters and brother."

"Mrs. Wollstonecraft had the skill of writing," Amelia said. "I know that well enough, Aunt Sophie, but I have no such skill."

"Ah, that was later. Do you know she once ran a school and from that experience came her first writings? My dear, it was difficult then but far simpler now."

"Open a school? Me? What do I know of schools?"

"All one must know," Aunt Sophie said. "You have your sisters for staff, you to teach reading, Berdine to teach religion, Clarisse to teach sewing, and

Daphne to teach French. You will take in small girls, say, under age eight—"

"Aunt Sophie! I couldn't!"

"Why not? It would be a day school, you see, so you needn't bother with boarding—"

"But who would send children—"

"Ah, there it is! I know just the house, and it is in a small village called Puddleafton near my country house, and it has never had a school—"

"But—"

"With my sponsorship it will be quite the thing to the minds of the village mothers."

Amelia's voice wavered. "You have already done too much. I cannot be in your debt. But perhaps, if it were understood between us that you must advance no money, but only help me to make the right contacts, and that I am to pay the rent on this house—"

Aunt Sophie leaned back, folded her jeweled hands in her lap, and smiled. "You will be a success, Amelia, because you are as stubborn as I."

Amelia clapped her hands together. Her eyes sparkled. "Do you know, Aunt Sophie, now that I think on it, I find the idea of a school most exciting! Is it not what I have done for years, teach ciphering and reading to young girls?"

"You do have experience with your sisters," Aunt Sophie agreed.

"And I would be supporting myself! And my sisters! It is more than I had ever dreamed possible."

"I am relieved that the idea pleases you, Amelia. I have ever thought you were a woman of spirit."

Amelia frowned, realizing that, although the founding of a school could open to her and her sisters a whole new future, its success depended on a suitable setting as much as on her own talents. The fear of losing such an exciting dream made her voice tremble. She asked, "But are you quite sure that a proper house is available?"

"Of course I am sure. Sir Richard Wyland owns half the village, including the house I have in mind, and I know that it is now unoccupied. With my intervention in your behalf, he could hardly refuse to accept you as a tenant."

CHAPTER 5

Although the sale of the house at Pickerton Cross removed the roof from over their heads, and the parlor furnishings from their ownership, the buyers seemed disinclined to claim the other furnishings. Indeed, so mismatched and overused were the bits of hand-down furniture in the morning room and bed-chambers that the buyers agreed Amelia could even keep the feather beds if she would remove the old furnishings.

By the time Amelia arrived in Pickerton Cross, Berdine had carefully packed the six and a half place settings that remained of their grandmother's por-celain, as well as their mismatched collection of blue ironstone, but had been unable to decide what else needed doing.

After Aunt Sophie's servants had arrived, packed up the rest, and removed it by wagon, Amelia and Berdine and Daphne went in Aunt Sophie's carriage directly from their empty house to their new lodgings in Puddleafton.

"Is it a grand house?" Daphne asked.

"I know nothing of it and must hope only that it has both roof and stove, as we lack such," Amelia said.

"Have you not seen the house, then?" Berdine inquired.

"No, I have not even seen the village."

"Then how did you acquire this place?"

"It belongs to a friend of Aunt Sophie's and she arranged that we should lease it from him."

"You do not know the owner?"

"I have met him," Amelia said. "He came to tea at Aunt Sophie's twice while I was there and I attended a party at his grandmother's home." She did not say aloud that she had looked for him at all the other parties, but he had not been there. In truth she had been relieved that he had not. Truly she had been relieved. She told herself over and over that she had been relieved because she had no reason to wish to see Sir Richard again.

When they were together, twice for tea and once to dance, he had seemed most friendly and interested in her. As she had no need of a man's interest and would only find it a complication in her life, she was relieved to discover that his interest had only been a matter of charming manners on his part. She told herself *that* several times, also.

That he was kind enough to allow her to rent a house that he owned was as generous as any act extended her by anyone, except Aunt Sophie, and with the edge of her father's debts darkening her horizons, she could not afford to be indebted to anyone herself.

Besides, she had quite enough to fill her worry-time. With no experience whatever, she must manage to open a school and earn support for herself and her sisters. The thought of it almost drove from her mind the question of what had become of Father. Where was he? True, his debts to date were paid and he would not be shadowed by gaolers, but she knew too well how quickly he could run up new debts.

No, until she heard from him, she must try not to worry about him and to concentrate, instead, on the school.

The March skies were as dull as unpolished pewter above the bare trees. She stared from the coach window at the passing farms, their stone fences dipping in frequent breaks, their pastures seas of mud. Forlorn sheep huddled together, an occasional loner wandering through a fence gap and standing rockstill at the side of the narrow road.

Twice the coachman had to stop and jump down to push one of the wandering sheep from the center of the road so that the carriage might pass. The animals remained where he left them, at the roadside, staring stupidly, showing no sign of fear of the horses or the carriage.

The road turned upward into low hills and between gray boulders to land unfit for tilling and even uninviting as pasture for larger animals, though Amelia supposed the sheep might graze anywhere. Because of the rising of the road, they were in Puddleafton before seeing it.

Its main street was cobbled and wound a slow curve, edged on one side by a swollen stream that rushed down from the higher hills. Its other side was lined with shops, their dull gray stone faces staring across the road and stream to a common that boasted a few small trees and paths and was circled by nearly identical stone cottages. No cottage boasted more than a main floor topped by a high-pitched roof. Narrow dormers broke the rooflines and chimney pots poured steady ribbons of yellow-gray coal smoke into the already gray sky.

Mud roads led away from the main road in several places. With no trees, except on the common, Amelia could see the rows of houses pressing towards the hills.

The coach turned across a bridge, rattled off its stones, and steadied on the muddy path. It stopped in front of one of the cottages that faced the common.

The coachman opened the door. "We are here, Miss Grant."

He helped them down, then turned to gather their trunks and valises from the carriage top.

"It has no proper garden," Daphne whispered.

"It faces the common. I am sure that will be quite pleasant," Berdine said. "And I see the church spire. It will be no walk at all."

"But it looks so small," Daphne said. "We'll not have near the room we had at Pickerton Cross."

Amelia said nothing. She pushed open the door, expecting cobwebs and mice.

Instead she found herself in a small entry hall facing a large sitting room. Too surprised to speak, she stepped inside. The room stretched the length of one side of the house, and on the inner wall between the doorways, a cozy fire blazed in the grate of a stone hearth. The outer walls, front, back, and side, were lined with narrow windows that let in a surprising amount of light for such a dull day. Their panes shone clean. The windowsills gleamed. The walls were white with fresh paint. A Welsh carpet, woven in bright reds and yellows, covered the floor. But to her greatest surprise, a large mahogany desk and chair stood at the far end of the room faced by three small tables and eight small chairs that had obviously been newly made of some pale wood.

"Is it all right, then, ma'am?" a voice said, and Amelia turned to see Dora standing in the far doorway, her white apron pulled askew on her striped poplin and her taffy hair slipping out from her cap. Her face was more flushed than usual.

"Dora! Why are you here?"

"Miss Stafford sent me, ma'am. Come along through. We've everything in place, though I've still the dishes to unpack. The wagons left only half an hour ago."

"We stopped at midday at an inn," Amelia said.

"Yes, miss, but the wagons came right through."

They followed Dora into a small dining room, its walls freshly whitewashed, its curtains starched. In its center stood their old table and chairs. The sideboard filled one wall. Beyond it were the kitchen and pantry and a small room with a cot and washstand and Dora's other dress on the wall peg.

"But, Dora, I cannot pay you wages," Amelia said.

"No bother, ma'am. Miss Stafford pays me by the year and, as she has me to spare, she's loaned me to you." Dora sounded defensive when she answered, "I'll be a help, ma'am, for I can cook and launder as well as clean, and this place is small enough for me to handle. You won't have time if you're to teach your school. You'll need me, ma'am."

"Oh, Dora! I am delighted to have you. In truth, none of us can cook or launder, but I had thought I might find a local daily."

"Might as well keep me," Dora said. "I'm paid for."

"And the school desks? Did Miss Stafford send them?"

"No, ma'am. The gentleman what owns the place did that and had the painting done and the new rugs."

"It's ever so much bigger from the inside," Daphne said. "But there aren't many rooms, are there?"

"Three bedchambers and a boxroom under the eaves, ma'am," Dora said. "Quite nice sized they are. The stairs are behind the door on the far side of the entry."

"And Miss Clarisse? Will she be here today?"

Dora pulled a folded notepaper from her pocket. "I near forgot. Miss Stafford said to give you this."

Amelia broke the seal and squinted at the spidery writing.

"Amelia, my dear," it said, "as I cannot believe that Clarisse will be of much use until you have students ready for their sewing instruction, I have made other plans for her, and I would consider it a favor if you would concur. A dear friend is traveling to Ireland for a short stay and required companionship beyond her maid. It seemed a godsent opportunity to expose Clarisse to more worldly behavior. Before you feel I have done my friend poorly, let me assure you that Lady Ethelwynne never ceases talking except to eat and sleep, so she will require of Clarisse only the ability to listen. Still, it may be that in listening, Clarisse will absorb some small understanding of social conversations. They shall be gone the summer, returning by autumn, and I have a distant hope that at that time I might try again to introduce Clarisse to suitable gentlemen. If, of course, you feel need of her, she could return to you at an earlier date, as my friend was primarily concerned with companionship during the crossing. If there is ought else you need, send word. I shall return to my country house in May. Some of your pupils shall have arrived by then. Yours with affection, dear Amelia, from your loving aunt."

Handing the letter to Berdine to read, Amelia sank into a chair at the dining table and stared blankly at the tea tray that Dora set before her. She was not disturbed that Clarisse had been sent to Ireland, knowing that Aunt Sophie would know better than herself what might be suitable for Clarisse, but she found the whole arranging of her affairs to have slipped so far beyond her control that she needed time to straighten out her thoughts.

Father had disappeared, Clarisse was off to Ireland with a titled lady, her new house came equipped with a gift of school furniture and Dora, and from somewhere pupils were to drop in like rainfall, making it possible for her to begin to repay the debts that she, herself, had somehow begun to contract.

She had five pounds in her reticule, and that alone, though a goodly sum to have in one place, was not sufficient to carry them for any time at all. Fortunately the buyers in Pickerton Cross had no interest in books, enabling her to bring away their library. It would suffice for now. But there were other supplies she must provide for a school and they must eat and pay the rent and purchase candles and soap and hire someone to do whatever one did to a garden. Without so much as the purchase of a bit of clothing, she would run up debts with the shop owners for their daily needs.

"I am delighted that Clarisse will have this opportunity to travel and broaden her mind," Berdine said, "but I am puzzled by this reference to conversation."

"I thought you would have found Clarisse a husband by now," Daphne said.

"It is much too difficult to explain," Amelia said, "and we still must unpack our trunks and sort our books."

"Not before we eat!" Daphne exclaimed. "Do stop dream-gazing, Amelia, and pour the tea."

Daphne bent above her plate, so intent on buttering her muffin that her blond curls fell forward to nearly hide her face. Berdine sat quietly, her round face composed, her small hands folded in her lap, waiting to be served. When a heavy knocking rattled the front door, neither of them turned, but Amelia set down the teapot and pushed back her chair.

"You pour, Berdine. I will answer the door."

"Answer the door?" Berdine said, surprised.

"We've only Dora in the kitchen now. There are many things we must learn to do for ourselves," Amelia said, and hurried through the sitting room to the entry.

She pulled it open, expecting that the carriage had returned with a forgotten valise or that a tradesman had come to show his wares. Instead, she stared, surprised, at her new landlord.

"Sir Richard!"

"Miss Grant," he said, and gave her a slight bow. "I have stopped to see that you have safely arrived and to request what you may need."

"That's most kind of you. I—I thought, of course, that you were in Bath."

"As your aunt no doubt mentioned, my country

house is nearby. I am much more often there than elsewhere."

Amelia noted his riding dress and saw past his shoulder to his horse tethered to a post by the road. She said, "We had just sat down for tea. Will you join us?"

He smiled, but the turning at his mouth's corners had an insolence that puzzled her. Not impertinence, really, but more as though he found her amusing.

"I think not, Miss Grant, but if you would step aside, perhaps I could come as far as the entryway to avoid the neighbors' stares."

"I am sorry!" Amelia exclaimed, and backed away. He followed her past the outer door but not into the sitting room, so that she found herself closeted with him in the very tiny hallway.

"You will have much to do, I am sure, so I have only stopped to ask, as your landlord, my dear, if there is ought found wanting. A roof leak, perhaps, or a loose floorboard?"

"That's kind, but surely you have an agent who handles your properties?" Amelia said.

"No." He shook his head and added, "I prefer to handle my own affairs and to know all my tenants."

"I see," Amelia said. "I had thought to seek out the agent within the next few days."

"Is there a problem, then?"

"No," she said, and chewed thoughtfully on her lower lip, unknowingly causing the dimple to twinkle at her mouth's lower edge. "I—I think I must then ask you, Sir Richard. Aunt Sophie was most vague about when my rent would be payable. I must know the date in order to properly order my affairs."

He shrugged and smiled down at her. "I would not

want you to worry about that, Miss Grant. I am in no dire needs for my funds."

"But I must know a date," she insisted.

"As it is payable yearly, you may pay as you choose before year's end," he said.

Her eyes widened. She had never before been a tenant, but she doubted that rents were thus paid. "Is that the way with all your properties?" she asked.

"Miss Grant, all my tenants love me, rest assured. With each I have a good understanding. I have put no widows on the curbings, so you must not think that I extend you some special privilege."

Amelia blinked, horrified to have her thoughts so clearly guessed.

He continued, "I hope the premises will suit. Miss Stafford thought it would, and she must be a better judge than I of your needs. If there is ought else, do let me know."

And before she could thank him for the desks and rugs, he was out the door. Amelia stepped onto the doorstep. He saw her and stopped by his horse, waiting.

"Sir Richard," she said, "I must thank you for the desks."

"The house is usually let furnished," he said. "But it was left in disrepair. I would have totally refurnished it for you, but your aunt said that was all you needed."

"Yes, it is fine," she said.

He nodded, mounted his horse, and turned away, leaving her to watch him ride down the road and across the bridge out of sight. He did not look back.

That he might have felt the need to repaint and refurbish the house for a new tenant she did not question, and that he might also include some furnishings she guessed was reasonable, but that he had no deadlines for the payment of rents she did not believe.

He was doing it as a favor because his grandmother was an old and dear friend of Amelia's great-aunt. She could not think why the idea upset her so, except that she had spent so many years trying to avoid debt. Now she found herself plunged into debts, not of her father's but of her own. Beyond the rent that she owed him, she was indebted for his generosity. She was indebted, it would seem, to her aunt and to the countess and to Sir Richard and probably to the lady who had unsuspectingly accepted Clarisse as a companion. And soon she would be in debt to every shopkeeper in Puddleafton.

She stamped her foot and closed the door with an unnecessary bang. "I won't," she said to herself, and her own voice in the entryway surprised her.

"Well, I won't," she said again. "It is bad enough to be in debt to shopkeepers, but I shall not be in debt to Aunt Sophie and all her friends. I am not her ward. I am quite capable of caring for myself and my sisters and I shall do so, so there, Sir Richard Wyland, and yours will be the first billing I shall pay as soon as I have earned a tuition."

Wandering back among the small tables of the sitting-room-turned-classroom, she frowned. But where were these tuitions to come from? How was she to find the students that Aunt Sophie had assured her would fill her school?

CHAPTER 6

The first three students did, indeed, drop like rainfall from the sky.

On the third day of their residence in Puddleafton, Mrs. Tupper, the greengrocer's wife, arrived with her two small daughters, aged four and five.

"You are the niece of Miss Stafford, I understand," she said, after Amelia had invited her into the schoolroom.

"My grandfather was Miss Stafford's brother," Amelia explained.

Mrs. Tupper stiffened. "Your grandfather was the baronet?"

"No, madam, he was a younger son."

Mrs. Tupper visibly relaxed, her shoulders dropping. "But you are related to the baronet, are you not?"

My goodness, Amelia thought, I do believe my school shall be filled with people who want gossip of Aunt Sophie's circle but are not within it to ask or of the servant class to overhear.

Aloud she said, "The baronet is my second cousin, but I have never met him."

She did not feel compelled to explain that as soon as the Staffords had realized the weaknesses of Amelia's father, they had disowned Amelia's mother, if not formally at least in spirit, and only Aunt Sophie had remained in communication, writing to their mother two or three times a year. After their mother's death, Aunt Sophie had swooped down upon them, possibly with some thought then of taking them home with her, but all Amelia remembered of that visit had been some very loud and prolonged arguments between her aunt and her father. Aunt Sophie had then disappeared from their lives, except for a yearly box of Christmas gifts that invariably contained gloves and reticules. She had reappeared four years ago to inform Amelia that, as she was then eighteen, Aunt Sophie was prepared to introduce her to Bath society.

Amelia had declined, unable to imagine leaving her responsibilities, but she had declined politely and with regret. Amelia's father, usually so mild, had turned quite violent, with words if not actions, and Amelia, when she realized that Aunt Sophie was easily his match, had fled the room.

Despite all, Miss Sophie Stafford had insisted on remaining their one link with the Staffords. Amelia did not and had never wished any further link with the family that had chosen to forget her mother.

Mrs. Tupper, however, found some enchantment in the link, because she enrolled her daughters on the spot.

The next day brought the local curate leading by the hand a girl of six years.

"This is my niece, Anne," he said, "my brother's child. She is orphaned and lives with me at the parish house. I have taught her to read, but the housekeeper has not the time to teach her other skills, and also,

I understand, you will include French language lessons."

"Indeed we shall, Mr. Measure," Amelia said.

"Then I am quite satisfied," he said, and looked about the room, but Amelia did not think he was noticing the furnishings and she could not imagine that he was inspecting the cleanliness.

"Is there something else I may show you?" she asked. "Perhaps our books?"

"No, no, I am satisfied, Miss Grant." The Reverend John Measure stood silent, his young face unnaturally solemn, Amelia thought, for there were laugh lines around his eyes and mouth and a boyish tilt to his nose. He was a small man and she thought it must be a constant effort for him to stand so straight in his dark garb and attempt to appear severe and pious.

"Then we shall look forward to Anne's presence when we begin instruction on Monday," Amelia said.

He started at her voice as though he had forgotten she was there, then said nervously, "Miss Grant, I—I met another lady, a Miss Berdine Grant, and it was she—that is—I understood—"

"Berdine is my sister," Amelia said. "She will instruct the students in religion and French. I did not know you had met."

"She—she stopped by the parish house to acquaint herself and offer her services to the church, which was most kind. Indeed, I felt remiss that she should call first, as I certainly meant to call when I heard this house was newly occupied."

"Only for four days, Mr. Measure. Your thoughtfulness is most appreciated. I shall tell my sister that you mentioned meeting her."

"Please do," he said eagerly, then drew himself up and added stiffly, "That is, do give her my regards and tell her that I shall look forward to seeing all the Grants at service on Sunday. If there is else I can do—"

"How kind," Amelia said, but thought for a fleeting moment that something other than kindness had prompted his offer. As she had so many other matters on her mind, though, the thought slipped by and was forgotten.

For the next week Amelia and Berdine bent their efforts to educating the Tupper girls and keeping up with young Anne Measure. While the Tupper children had not so much as learned to curl their chubby fingers around charcoal sticks, and had apparently never been shown a book with pictures in it, thin little Anne, with her pale hair pulled back into a clumsy braid, could not be tempted away from the books. She tolerated silently the instructions, but when Amelia tried to play a few games or allowed the girls time to draw pictures, Anne stole away to hide behind the door and bury her nose in a book.

"She reads amazingly well for a child of six," Berdine said, as she stooped to retrieve a book left on the floor in Anne's hiding place.

Amelia closed the door behind the departing children and returned to the schoolroom. "Yes, but she cannot write legibly and she is slow to cipher."

"Do you remember how it was with us after Mother died?" Berdine asked.

Amelia nodded, remembering well how they had lost themselves in reading the forbidden novels that they found in their mother's wardrobe, gaining escape from their sorrow. Perhaps it would do no harm to let Anne remain behind the door with a book for part of each day.

"It must be difficult for the curate to raise a girl," Berdine added.

Amelia said, "Do you know, I believe he braids her hair and buttons her dress. The buttons were mismatched today and I cannot think the housekeeper would be so poor at combing."

Berdine said, "He seems very kind."

"Kind!" Amelia exclaimed. "I think that's quite amazing. Father certainly never buttoned a button for any of us."

When Berdine did not reply, Amelia looked up from the slate she was cleaning and was surprised to see that Berdine was blushing. As she could think of no reason for it, she decided Berdine must be overwarm from exertion and suggested she go to the kitchen for a drink of something cool and a rest. Without answering, Berdine fled.

Amelia shook her head and returned to her task, rubbing with a rag to remove the chalk marks from the slate. This was their second week of instruction and yet the Tupper children could not print their ABC's. They had, however, learned to count and mastered color names. Tomorrow she would have Daphne start them on some simple stitching.

And where was Daphne? As she and Berdine could well handle three small girls, Amelia had not needed Daphne in the classroom, but she had been busy enough that she had forgotten to notice where Daphne spent her time.

A rapping on the door distracted her. Amelia hurried to answer, then drew back in surprise to see Sir Richard Wyland, an elegantly dressed woman, and a small girl with bright red curls standing on her doorstep.

For a moment she wished there were some way she could turn back time, have seen who approached through a window and called Dora to answer. The disdain on the woman's face showed clearly what she thought of people who opened their own doors.

Amelia led them into the schoolroom, regretting for the first time that she had no separate parlor. When Sir Richard introduced Amelia to his house-guests, the Marchioness of Darmerdavin and her eight-year-old daughter, Lady Isabelle, Amelia knew that she could not invite a marchioness to pull up a chair at the dining table.

Sensing that, Sir Richard said quickly, "Miss Grant, Lady Isabelle shall be your student."

Amelia stared, uncomprehending. A marquess's daughter would be instructed at home by a governess.

"That is satisfactory, is it not?" Lady Darmerdavin said.

"But—yes, if you wish, madam," Amelia stuttered. "You—you do understand that I have only day students here, local village girls?"

"I have been assured that the instruction you offer is quite exceptional," the marchioness said. "My daughter has her own governess, of course, but she is unexceptional, I think, and Sir Richard assures me that a month or two of instruction in your school will polish Lady Isabelle's French grammar."

If the marchioness wished her daughter's grammar polished, why not send for a Frenchwoman to teach her, Amelia wondered, but as she could not ask, she nodded agreement and watched in silence as Sir Richard excused them and hastened them away. He did not, however, hasten them quickly enough. They were halfway to the carriage when Amelia discovered what had become of Daphne.

From around the side of the house appeared a tall, mud-streaked young person, her skirts caught up to expose oversized workman's boots, her hair wrapped in a scarf of red cotton that half covered her face. The portion of the face that showed was so dirt caked as to hide completely the creamy complexion.

Her identity did not occur to Amelia until Sir Richard bowed in the direction of the tool-carrying apparition and said, "Good day, Miss Daphne."

"Do I know you?" Daphne said flatly, not noticing the fine carriage with the crest of the marquess on its side.

Sir Richard laughed and Amelia shrank back into the shadows of the doorway at recognition of her sister's voice. He said, "Not yet, perhaps, but I should know you anywhere, for your aunt informed me that you were a younger version of Miss Clarisse."

Daphne laughed back at him and said, "A muddier version."

"On you, dear lady, even mud is becoming," he said, and stepped into the carriage.

When the carriage had completely disappeared from view, Amelia stepped onto the path and demanded, "Daphne, what are you doing?"

Daphne looked up from the hole she was digging in the mud and said, "I am preparing the garden."

"The garden? Explain yourself, please."

Wiping a muddy hand across her eyes, Daphne stood still and said, "Now, Amelia, don't scold. You said yourself we can't afford to pay wages, and you and Berdine don't need me in the schoolroom, so I've wandered about a bit and talked to a person or two and I have learned that it is not difficult to plant a garden. One need only turn the soil now so that it is ready for the seeds next month. I've already marked out the vegetable rows at the rear of the house and now I am planning a few flowers for the front."

"You have lost your mind!" Amelia exclaimed.

"No, it is not difficult and it will cost nothing because I've been given ever so many seeds—"

"Who gave you seeds? Who told you how to make a garden?" Amelia demanded.

"I—I watched the yardman at home, Amelia," Daphne faltered, then set her chin as firmly as her sister's and said, "and I've walked around the village and talked to a gardener or two. They didn't mind explaining and they gave me seeds."

"You've been talking to strange workingmen in other people's gardens?" Amelia asked, so stunned by this new situation that she could not even muster anger. She had told her sister many things, but among them she supposed she had never thought to tell her not to talk to strange gardeners.

"It's all right," Daphne said. "You need not fear embarrassment, Amelia. I have never told them my name, so no doubt they think I am a scullery maid. And it is ever so much fun, Amelia, it truly is. Would you like to come and dig a bit?"

Amelia clapped her hands over her mouth to hold back the torrent of words that longed to be poured out. Her thoughts were so disconnected, swinging from Daphne's behavior to Sir Richard's obvious amusement, that she knew that no matter what she said, it would not come out quite the way she meant it.

Scullery maid, indeed. Sir Richard had known exactly who Daphne was, without a moment's hesitation, despite her filthy clothing and grimy hands and face. What could he have thought? And why had he laughed?

And why had he brought the Lady Isabelle to a village day school?

For that matter, why were the marchioness and her daughter staying at his estate at all?

CHAPTER 7

If the first students appeared like raindrops, the next weeks provided a deluge. Word swept the village of the enrollment of a Lady Isabelle, daughter of a marquess, and within two days of her arrival Amelia found herself in the amazing position of turning away students.

Altogether she accepted twelve girls, knowing she could handle no more.

"We shall have more than we can do, Daphne," she told her young sister firmly, "so you may return your boots and tools to the garden shed, scrub the mud from your fingernails, and join Berdine and myself."

"I should much prefer to tend the garden," Daphne complained as she buttered her third muffin.

"The outdoor air gives you too great an appetite. It will cost me less to hire a yardman," Amelia snapped.

Daphne glared back. "I will not teach stitching."

Berdine said softly, "The devil finds work for idle hands."

"Yes," Daphne retorted, "and he calls it *stitching*."

Berdine folded her hands, lowered her eyes, and

79

said gently, "Daphne, dear, stitching is one of a woman's finest accomplishments. It teaches patience and perseverence."

Around a mouthful of muffin, Daphne said, "*You* teach the children patience and perseverence, Berdine. If I must remain in the classroom, at least allow me to teach sums or French."

"Certainly I shall not depend on you to teach table deportment," Amelia said.

Daphne pushed back an errant curl, leaving a smudge of jam on her golden hair, then said, "I shall teach because I wish to do my share, but in return you must agree not to hire a gardener."

"What? Leave the garden a sea of weeds?"

"The garden must be mine, Amelia. I shall tend it after the children leave for their homes each day."

Berdine said, "It is not done, Daphne."

Daphne laughed, pushed back her chair, and stood, stretching her arms above her head to loosen her back as though she were in the privacy of her bedchamber. Her gray poplin frock strained at the seams, reminding Amelia that she could no longer clothe Daphne in hand-downs. The child was as tall as Amelia, and though her figure had only begun to show soft curves, her shoulders were wide and straight. The red sash she had added to the plain gown hung from its stitching below her bosom, the ties half undone at her back. Amelia could not be sure if Daphne's creamy complexion was merely unwashed or had already begun to sun-darken.

Daphne said, "I shall promise to wear an apron and a servant's cap when I am in the front garden, if that would please you, Berdine, and you may tell passersby that I am the gardener's daughter."

"I should prefer that you wore a sunbonnet and gloves," Amelia sighed, but she doubted that Daphne heard because she had run out through the kitchen and pantry, letting the garden door bang shut.

"What is to be done?" Berdine asked softly.

Amelia said, "I do remember that the vicar's wife at Pickerton Cross did both sowing and weeding in her garden."

"But she did not dig in the soil with a spade!" Berdine exclaimed. "Daphne lifts her foot and puts it on the spade! She ties up her skirt!"

"She is also very proficient at sums and French," Amelia said, her voice firm. As she felt quite sure that she could not change Daphne's behavior, she chose the easier path of accepting Daphne's faults with her virtues, hoping Berdine would do the same.

Berdine folded her hands in her lap and lowered her eyes. Amelia wondered if Berdine was praying for Daphne's reputation or for Amelia to be more firm with their young sister.

The rearrangement of responsibilities worked smoothly, despite Berdine's fears. Berdine and Amelia taught the eight older girls in the schoolroom. The children sat at their desks, their hair tied back with ribbons, their poplin frocks hidden beneath prim white aprons, their slippered feet wiggling quietly. Daphne took the four younger girls to the dining room and, with her own special magic, taught them sums as well as bits of French conversation. Intrigued by their progress, Amelia often stood near the door to listen.

Daphne sang in her lilting voice,

One and two is three,
Regardez vous, merci!
Three and one is four,
S'il vous plait, encore!

Whenever Amelia glanced out the window and saw Daphne with her skirt caught up in her apron strings to clear her boot tops and her sunbonnet pushed back to hang uselessly by its ribbons, she reminded herself that Daphne had managed to teach the Tupper girls their alphabet.

When Daphne plunked herself down at the dining table one afternoon and began to confide the village gossip, Amelia was forced to remark, "Is there no end to your talents?"

Had Berdine been with them, she might have felt required to correct Daphne, but as Berdine had decided to walk Anne Measure to the parish house so that she could deliver a jar of jam, Amelia relaxed and prepared to enjoy Daphne's tales. She poured them each their tea, slid the plate of cakes nearer to her young sister, and even offered her more butter.

"I can close my eyes but I cannot close my ears," Daphne pointed out. "It concerns Sir Richard."

"Oh! That is beyond village gossip! I think you should not repeat—ah—whatever you may have heard. And from whom would you hear talk of Sir Richard?"

"It was the laundress in the next garden talking with the housemaid," Daphne admitted. "But you are correct, I must not repeat tattle." She concentrated on buttering her cake, her head bent forward so that her curls hid her face.

Amelia chewed her lip in frustration.

Daphne looked up, her eyes sparkling with mischief.

"Tell me," Amelia sputtered.

"They say the marchioness far prefers Sir Richard's estate to her own, though her own is larger and her husband wealthier."

"Oh, that is tattle! You were right, you should not have repeated it and we must both forget it," Amelia said. "I do not care for that sort of talk at all. Tell me, rather, shall the Tuppers' niece have a large wedding party?"

Having turned Daphne's chatter to village matters, Amelia settled back, her teacup cradled in her hands, her smile fixed on her face, while her mind wandered.

Was it true? Did the marchioness remain as Sir Richard's guest for something less than social reasons? Were there other guests in his house? Could Sir Richard be involved in intentions that were less than honorable?

His grandmother had said that he did not plan to wed again now that he had an heir. Aunt Sophie said that Richard's marriage had been a duty match to the daughter of his father's closest friend. Both hinted that he preferred to now remain single. Was that why he chose a married woman as his guest? Was she more than a mere guest?

But that was quite mad to consider! How could she, Amelia, possibly know who stayed at Richard's estate or why they were invited or what their behavior? It did not concern her. It was truly tattle. No doubt the marquess was a close friend of Richard and there were other guests at the estate that kept Lady Darmerdavin there.

"I'll go to the door," Daphne said, jumping from her place.

Amelia started, not having heard the knock. As Daphne ran through the rooms and opened the street door, Amelia leaned forward, straining to hear who it might be. Not another mother with a child to enroll, she hoped, as she disliked turning them away. In truth she could allow one more, as Lady Isabelle of the red curls had appeared only once last week and once this week, so that Amelia had not had to spend any time instructing her, but still, her place was paid for and perhaps she would come more often in future.

Daphne flitted through the doorway. As she slid sideways, she left in view the tall young man who followed her.

Lord Pendarvin bowed. Before Amelia could speak or rise, he said, "Miss Daphne has invited me to tea, ma'am. I hope you will not object."

Rising, Amelia said, "You are most welcome. I fear we are a bit informal, as we have used the parlor for our schoolroom." Popping her head around the kitchen door, she asked Dora to bring another setting, then returned to her chair.

He said, "I have not taken tea at table since my nursery days. Top rate, I'd say. None of that balancing cups and plates on one's knee."

When Dora entered with the additional ironstone, she stopped still in the doorway and said, "Oh."

"Come in, Dora," Amelia said.

"Yes, ma'am. Oh, ma'am! Shall I bring the porcelain?" Dora's face flushed beneath her white cap frill.

"No," Amelia said, reaching out for the cup from

Dora's trembling hand. She inspected it and was relieved to see that, although it was one of their mismatched blue bits, at least it had no chips on the rim. She quite understood Dora's thinking. She should serve a viscount with porcelain. But would it not seem strange to offer his tea in a white porcelain service while she and Daphne drank from blue ironstone?

If Pendarvin noticed Dora's dismay, it did not show on his face. He leaned toward Amelia, saying softly, "What a thunderclap to meet your Miss Daphne! Couldn't believe it! She looks a young twin to Miss Clarisse!"

"I am sorry you have missed Clarisse, my lord. She is traveling with a friend of my aunt."

He took the cup from her hand and looked into her eyes, his own dark eyes solemn. "I did not come to Puddleafton expecting to see Miss Clarisse. I knew she was traveling."

"Oh? You have come on business matters, then?"

"No, ma'am. I have no children or borrowed children to enroll in your school," he blurted, then added, "That is, I never meant—ah—I called to see if you were comfortably set. If there's ought I can offer, say it out."

"How kind of you," Amelia said, and wondered what he meant by *borrowed children*.

"Do you live near here, then?" Daphne asked.

"Closer to Bath," he admitted, "but I have friends out this direction."

"Sir Richard Wyland?" Daphne asked.

"Daphne!" Amelia exclaimed.

The viscount said, "Ah—yes, miss—known Wyland forever."

"There is a marchioness visiting him," Daphne said, and Amelia blushed but remained silent.

"She's there herself?" he exclaimed.

"Her daughter attends our school," Daphne said.

"I'd heard somesuch," he admitted, "but I didn't know the marchioness was still—ah—tell me, Miss Daphne, do you teach, also?"

"I teach the younger children their sums and French."

"Aren't you clever! Never could manage French and I'm no shoot-up at sums, either."

Rather overwhelmed by his compliments, Daphne forgot what little discretion she ever had and blurted, "I also tend the garden!"

When Amelia accompanied the viscount to the door, she thought she could see through his eyes the smallness of the house, the simplicity of the furnishings, and her own slightly faded favorite frock, its ruffled collar comfortable but quite out of fashion. He would recognize them now for what they were, the very poorest sort of gentry, not the kind of people from whom he might choose a wife. No matter how Aunt Sophie might polish and fashion Clarisse, the viscount would recall the shabby house and shabby sisters as Clarisse's background.

"I must apologize for Daphne," Amelia said. "I fear I have let her be too free."

Pendarvin bent over her hand, startling her as he had the first time, but at least now she knew what he meant to do and was able to remain reserved. His lips touched her fingers.

He smiled and said softly, "I find her grand, but you surpass them all."

Then, to Amelia's surprise, a flush of color rose to his temples. He turned and hurried out the door.

Amelia stood in the entryway wondering what he could have meant by that. Perhaps the phrase was all he could recall, a line taught him by whichever tutor had taught him to bow and kiss a lady's hand. Now that he had seen their poverty, he certainly would not wish to call again.

Despite Aunt Sophie's insistence on his dislike of social gatherings, he had been raised in a world of servants and formality. His judgments would be thus molded. What a pity he had not met Berdine, the one sister whose manners were exemplary.

Yet perhaps by summer's end Clarisse, too, would know the behavior of a lady and would manage to uphold her share of a social conversation. If so, and if Aunt Sophie could arrange to draw Clarisse and the viscount together, Amelia's hopes for Clarisse might still be realized.

Amelia comforted herself with that thought until the letter arrived to tell her otherwise.

CHAPTER 8

"My dearest Amelia," Aunt Sophie wrote, "it seems that I have quite misjudged the ability of Clarisse to manage at this time to conduct herself with a degree of sophistication. As painful as I find this letter to write, I must proceed to tell you that my friend Lady Ethelwynne did not find the companionship of Clarisse to be completely to her satisfaction. Though she seemed genuinely fond of Clarisse, most unfortunately some lack of knowledge in Clarisse has led to an embarrassment that we could not expect Lady Ethelwynne to tolerate in a member of her party. As there is no way to put this delicately, I must be straight out and say that Clarisse, while on the journey and again after their arrival, lacked the discretion one might have wished and showed a regrettable incapacity for forebearance. Need I explain further? I think not. Feeling certain that Clarisse will mend her ways under your careful guidance, my dear, I remain, your devoted aunt."

Amelia folded the letter and tucked it away in her desk, doubting that she would need refer to it further, as it said nothing to enlighten her. Think as she might, she could not imagine what Clarisse might have done to so displease Lady Ethelwynne. Had she stood about with her mouth agape? If so, Aunt Sophie would not have been surprised and could surely have put such description to paper.

What Clarisse might have done that Aunt Sophie preferred not to commit to writing eluded Amelia. She sat at her desk, her chin in her hands, her brow creased with worry, until Dora called out that Miss Sophie's carriage had arrived.

Amelia ran to the door, brushing nervously at her dark muslin skirt. To her relief only the coachman came up the walk, carrying Clarisse's trunk, followed by a blank-faced Clarisse and a housemaid.

"Take the trunk up the stairs, if you will," Amelia said.

"Yes, Miss Grant."

While his boots thumped up the narrow staircase, Amelia and Clarisse threw their arms about each other, then stood apart, holding hands but not speaking. The scent of rain-washed air filled the entry hall. Clarisse was wrapped in a new bonnet and pelisse, both of a dull brown that might have suited Berdine but somehow made Clarisse appear pale, as though she had been ill, and cast shadows about her eyes.

"Is there other I may do, Miss Grant?" the coachman said, returning to the hall.

Amelia suggested that he and the maid take refreshment in the kitchen with Dora, but he declined, saying they had eaten at midday and were now hurried to return to Bath.

When they were gone, Amelia drew Clarisse up the stairs and to the bedchamber, removed her cloak, and settled her in the wing chair by the window. Clarisse turned her face toward the glass and gazed sadly at the road that wound from Puddleafton to the distant hills.

"Are you ill, dear?" Amelia asked.

"No, Amelia."

"Was Lady Ethelwynne unkind to you?"

"No," Clarisse whispered, but her lower lip quivered.

"She was unkind!" Amelia cried, jumping from the bed's edge and hurrying to catch Clarisse's limp hands in her own. "My darling, you should have sent word to me! You were not required to remain with her."

Tears brimmed in Clarisse's large eyes, then slid slowly from the corners, gliding down her creamy cheeks.

She gave a loud sniff.

"Clarisse, dearest, look at me! You must tell me what happened."

"You would not understand," Clarisse said. "Aunt Sophie was quite cross."

"Of course I shall understand," Amelia said. "It was Aunt Sophie's error if she allowed you to accompany an unsuitable woman. She need not blame you."

Clarisse caught up the hem of her gown and wiped away the tears from her face, then rubbed at her nose with her small fist. Amelia handed her a handkerchief. She waited silently while Clarisse blew her nose and settled her nerves. Gazing down at her, Amelia wondered who had so changed her sister. Clarisse's soft curls were brushed high onto her head and caught in a coil that made her look older than her years. Her rosy complexion was faded to white and she seemed thinner.

90

"Have you been ill?" Amelia asked.

"No."

"Then tell me what has happened."

"I—I—" Clarisse stammered, then suddenly cried out, "They are quite wrong! He is a fine gentleman and they judge him unfairly!"

Amelia sank back on the bed, confused, but attempting to retain her calm. "Who is a fine gentleman?" she asked.

"Mr.—Mr. Edmond Chicore," Clarisse whispered.

"And where did you meet this Mr. Chicore?"

"I—he was on the boat over to Ireland. It was—it was a rough passage."

"I hear it often is," Amelia said, biting back the questions that flooded her mind. If she pressed too hard, Clarisse would withdraw into numbed silence, she knew from experience.

"Lady Ethelwynne was quite ill. She went to her cabin but did not wish me with her. Do you know, Amelia, one feels ever so much better if one remains on deck to take the air?" Clarisse said, and looked up. For the first time a flicker of life brightened her expression.

"Indeed, I have heard."

"Yes, so that is what I did, I stood upon the deck and then Mr. Chicore was so kind. He walked with me." She stopped, as though that quite explained everything, and smiled.

"That was kind," Amelia agreed, "but who is Mr. Chicore?"

"He is a merchant, Amelia. He is in dry goods. He travels sometimes in his business."

"Ah. A merchant. And you met him on the boat."

Amelia smiled back, but inside she was frowning in her effort to guess the rest of the tale. "Did you see him again?"

"Yes."

"And where was that?"

"But you cannot imagine!" Clarisse suddenly exclaimed. "I was so surprised! Mr. Chicore lodged very near the estate where Lady Ethelwynne took me. And when I walked alone in the garden while my lady rested, there he was! Imagine!"

Amelia could not imagine. "This, this merchant had been invited to the home of Lady Ethelwynne's friends?"

"Invited? I—I do not think he ever met them. He merely came to the garden."

"To the garden. When you were there. I see. And did you see him after that?"

"Yes, daily," Clarisse said, her eyes glowing and the color creeping back into her cheeks. "He came morning and afternoon when I took the air."

"You walked out alone twice each day?"

"I was within the garden. Lady Ethelwynne thought it quite a good idea as she was busy with her friends. Indeed, she said that a young person needed air. She said it until she—until she saw Mr. Chicore!" Dissolving into tears, Clarisse buried her face in her skirts, crushing the cloth between her fingers.

Amelia waited. When Clarisse had quieted, she asked, "And why should the sight of a merchant annoy her so? Could she not simply tell him to go away?"

Clarisse glanced up and cried, "Oh, Amelia, he is so beautiful! You cannot imagine!"

"Mr. Chicore is beautiful? He is a young man, I presume?"

"Yes," Clarisse sobbed, "and I—I—I—love him!"

"Oh, my lord!" Amelia murmured, then waited for Clarisse to quiet. She said slowly, "Clarisse, did you ever leave the garden with Mr. Chicore?"

Clarisse shook her head and cried, "I shall never see Edmond again!"

"There, hush, I am sure it is all for the best," Amelia said, absentmindedly adding, "Were you but walking in the garden when Lady Ethelwynne saw you?"

There was a long silence during which Amelia forced her imagination to remain under control, knowing that Clarisse had no imagination and was not truly capable of misbehavior. Still, one could not know of what Mr. Edmond Chicore was capable.

Slowly Clarisse said, "He—he was holding my hand."

"And that angered her ladyship so much that she sent you home?"

"He—perhaps—I think she saw—he did kiss me, Amelia, but only on the brow."

Amelia stood and smoothed a tendril back from Clarisse's wet cheek. "I am glad you are here," she said. "We need you in the schoolroom, dear. Come along now, and I shall show you the house. It is really quite comfortable. Daphne and Berdine are at the shops but they shall be back soon for tea."

Clarisse stood to follow her and Amelia could see that she had indeed lost weight. "Dora will fix whatever you like, dear. What would tempt you most, Clarisse? Cake? Muffins? We have some honey."

Amelia started down the stairs, her hands touching the rails mounted on the walls of the enclosed stairway.

Clarisse said, "I could not eat."

Amelia turned and gazed up at her sister, now a silhouette against the bright, lace-framed window. "Indeed, try, dear."

"I shall never eat again," Clarisse wailed. "I shall never see Edmond again, so what may it matter?"

Daphne came dashing through the front door, flinging it open so that it banged against the wall, while Clarisse and Amelia stood on the stairs. On one arm Daphne carried her market basket, filled with small parcels of thread and ribbon and a ginger-bread cake from the baker's shop, while with her free hand she hoisted high her skirt, exposing slender ankles. Her bonnet hung from its strings, her curls slipped wildly away from their ribbons, and her face was flushed.

"I saw Aunt Sophie's carriage leaving the village!" she cried. "I ran all the way! So it is you, Clarisse, you are home at last!"

Dropping her basket, Daphne rushed up the stairs, pushing past Amelia, and caught Clarisse in her arms.

"Oh, Daphne!" Clarisse cried, and immediately burst anew into tears.

"I am so joyous to see you," Daphne said, "but I do not think we need weep about it." Turning, she started back down the stairs, her hand firmly holding Clarisse's hand. "Come along, Clarisse, you must see our house. It is ever so nice and it has quite a large back garden where I shall tend a proper kitchen garden and you shall help me, if you like. I do hope you will not go away again."

Daphne paused in the hallway to dig into her market basket and pull out her small, knitted reticule. From it she produced a twist of paper. "More seeds!" she said triumphantly, her blue eyes shining, her cheeks glowing pink. "And you needn't fuss, Amelia, because dear Mr. Measure himself gave them to me. One can hardly disapprove a gift from a man of the cloth, now, can one?"

"You saw Mr. Measure today?" Amelia asked.

"Yes. Oh." Daphne's smile faded and she turned away quickly, saying lightly, "I must take this cake to Dora for our tea. Doesn't it smell heavenly? The whole village smells of gingerbread today, I do believe. You will love the village, Clarisse. It has not *many* shops but it has some very *pleasant* shops."

"When did you see Mr. Measure?" Amelia persisted, managing, by stepping swiftly into the doorway that separated the entry from the schoolroom, to block Daphne.

Daphne glanced at Clarisse, then at the outer door, then at Amelia. "We did stop but a moment at the parish house," she said. "Berdine—Berdine had some sort of—a book, I think it was, yes, a book she wished to leave for Anne."

"Berdine was with you?"

"Yes, but yes, of course she was," Daphne said. "Why should I—ah, yes, Berdine was with me, Amelia."

That was suitable, Amelia thought. Had Daphne been wandering alone to the parish house, or to any of the houses, to beg seeds or chat alone with the gardeners, it would definitely be time to speak firmly to Daphne again. She had behaved well recently, staying in their own garden, or at least Amelia thought she had. One could not keep a constant eye on a fourteen-year-old girl.

"Did Mr. Measure himself give you the seeds?" Amelia asked, leading the way to the dining table. She paused in the schoolroom to point out to Clarisse its use and advantages. Clarisse nodded without speaking, her eyes averted, her cheeks tear stained.

While Daphne took the gingerbread to Dora, Amelia led Clarisse around the dining room, pointing out their old furnishings and familiar crockery, hoping Clarisse would find these reminders of their childhood home a comfort. Clarisse merely nodded, looking not a whit comforted.

It was not until later, after Dora had rushed from the kitchen to welcome Clarisse, and after Amelia had finally completed her description of the house and school to Clarisse, that Amelia remembered the seeds.

"I am surprised to hear of Mr. Measure's interest in the garden," she said. "Clarisse, dear, we have the most pleasant curate. His niece attends our school."

Clarisse did not so much as nod. She stared, wide eyed, at the window and a tear quivered on her long dark lashes.

Amelia hurried on, "And does the curate oversee the garden of the parish house, Daphne?"

"I don't think so," Daphne said.

"But then, why should he have seeds for you?"

"Oh, the seeds. Ah, it wasn't Mr. Measure. It was the housekeeper who gave me the seeds. She said the gardener had saved them for me, you see."

"Oh? You saw the housekeeper? Mr. Measure was not there?"

"Yes, he was," Daphne said. "He sent me through to the kitchen to ask—that is, he said that he was sure that the housekeeper would have extra seeds if I but asked. That is, I would not have *asked*, Amelia, truly I would not, but Mr. Measure did insist that I should," she said, her voice firm, then added weakly, "He knows of my interest in the garden, you understand."

"That was kind of him," Amelia said, once more puzzled. She knew there was something in Daphne's explanation that needed further examination, but she could not quite sort it out. Still, if Berdine had been with Daphne, it must all be proper. "Berdine. Daphne, where is Berdine? Did you run home and leave her alone at the shops?"

"Indeed, I did not!" Daphne exclaimed. "I would do no such thing."

"Then where is she?"

"She—" Daphne paused, a small frown creasing her brow, then said slowly, "I am afraid I did forget her."

"You left her at the village and forgot her? You forgot her where? How could you forget your sister?"

"It is not—I did not—Oh, it was quite simple, Amelia, that is, Berdine sent me on to the shops to purchase the sewing bits we needed and said I might look in at the baker's shop and choose a sweet for our tea. Afterwards, I was to stop back for her. But when I saw Aunt Sophie's carriage, I quite forgot to stop for Berdine before running home."

It was too much. Between them all, with their

variety of problems and aggravations, Amelia felt her mind would soon desert her. She caught Daphne's arm and said, "Daphne! Tell me straight away! Where is Berdine?"

In a small voice Daphne said, "She is with the curate. She—He invited her to stay and talk with him a bit."

"And she told you to go on alone for the errands?" Amelia asked, unbelieving.

"It was only across the road, Amelia. I have gone alone to the shops before," Daphne said.

Amelia's thoughts whirled. Certainly Daphne had gone alone to the shops and about the village. In a place as small as Puddleafton, it was quite safe. It was not Daphne who now caught Amelia by surprise. Of Daphne she had come to expect anything. But Berdine? Amelia had presumed that she had one sister about whom she need not fret, one sister who had complete understanding of responsibility, expectations, and the best behavior.

To be sure she had not misunderstood, she asked, "Has Berdine sent you alone to the shops before today?"

"Yes," Daphne said, "I am quite capable, you see."

"And Berdine remained with the curate?"

"Yes, but I never before forgot to stop back for her at the parish house. Perhaps I had best go now for her."

"Perhaps you had," Amelia said, wishing desperately that Aunt Sophie were at her country home instead of still in Bath. Until now Amelia had preferred to manage her own life. Now she felt that she was not managing at all, that in some way much of what she had thought she controlled was slipping away from her. She definitely needed a sensible adviser with whom to discuss the confusions that beset her.

CHAPTER 9

Although Sir Richard Wyland was not quite what
Amelia had had in mind when she desired an older,
wiser adviser, that is what she got.

She was standing in the front garden, surveying
the well-turned mud of Daphne's efforts, when he
rode up and tied his horse to the front post. Afternoon sunlight glinted off the golden-brown sheen of
his thick hair. Had he picked his leather riding coat
to match his hair? The thought whisked through
Amelia's mind and she angrily brushed it away, telling herself that Sir Richard's appearance was not her
concern. Still, one would needs be blind not to notice
the tall, romantic figure he cut in his brown coat,
fawn breeches, and gleaming boots. Laugh lines
wreathed his slender, tanned face, crinkling the outer
corners of his warm eyes.

"Ah, surveying the estate, are you, Miss Grant?"
he called as he hurried toward her.

"I have no notion what I survey," she admitted.
"I am totally baffled. Is it true that all one need do
is turn over the earth and drop in seeds in order to
produce a garden?"

Sir Richard studied the earth. Amelia noticed now

that it seemed to have some sort of lines on its surface, as though it had been combed by a giant.

"Perhaps it is not quite that simple," he said, "but I fancy that Daphne knows what she is about. It all looks very properly prepared. However, I must apologize and do so profusely. There is no reason why your young sister should do this work. It is obviously my responsibility and I shall tend to it. My gardener and his helpers will arrive tomorrow."

"Oh, dear, I think not, though I should rather prefer it, Sir Richard," Amelia sighed. "I have promised Daphne that she may have the gardening to herself. Any change in that arrangement would have to be made with Daphne."

"How charming," Sir Richard said. "I wish I lived across the common so that I might watch the young lady."

Amelia gasped. "Oh, my! That is what I feared! It is quite unsuitable, is it not, for her to tend the garden?"

"In Puddleafton I think you need not worry yourself," Sir Richard said. "I did not intend to imply any such meaning. Daphne is not the first female to find joy in nature, I assure you, and in these parts such women are rather admired."

"Admired as eccentrics," Amelia complained.

"No, no, dear Miss Grant, rather they are called originals, and even in stuffy London, a true original is valued."

As Amelia could think of no reply to such a statement, she said instead, "Is there some problem that brings you here, Sir Richard?"

"Problem? None whatsoever. I was passing through the village and thought I would stop by. I did hear that Miss Clarisse had returned and intended to ask after her health. I hope she is not ill?"

"Clarisse is well, thank you. I regret she is not in. My sisters are out calling. One matter puzzles me, Sir Richard, though no doubt the explanation is quite simple. Although the tuition has been paid for Lady Isabelle, we seldom see her. If her mother has decided that the instruction I have to offer is not, after all, suitable, I do feel I should return the money."

"Do no such thing!" he exclaimed. "The child should be in attendance. Indeed, I thought she was! When I offered to deliver her to you myself, her mother assured me that she had made all arrangements with her own coachman and maid. Certainly I shall inquire into the matter."

There was a fierceness in his voice that surprised Amelia. She did not question further and he seemed satisfied to change the subject to the weather, the condition of the roof, and other empty nonessentials, so that when he left a few minutes later, she was as confused as ever as to the purpose of his visit.

To her amazement and Daphne's delight, his visits thereafter occurred on a daily basis as he delivered in his coach the red-haired Lady Isabelle. Not only did he ride with her, he walked to the door with her. As Amelia had been led to believe from her visit in Bath that the gentlemen of the *ton* seldom stirred from their private chambers before noon, she found her opinions of Sir Richard undergoing a drastic change.

She had satisfied herself that he was unsuitable as a prospective husband for either of her sisters in that Aunt Sophie had admitted that he was partial to the gaming tables. She would not have Clarisse or Berdine married to a gambler. Their mother had suffered quite enough from such a fate. And then she had heard the rumors, as sincerely as she tried to ignore them, of the women in his life, rumors she could not ignore once she had met the marchioness. They confirmed Aunt Sophie's theory that Richard was not interested in marriage and confirmed Amelia's belief that even if he was, no sensible woman would bind herself to such a man, for he seemed of questionable character. She could not bring herself to call him a rake, but she suspected others did.

Yet here he was early each morning escorting small Lady Isabelle to school, then stopping to discuss gardening with Daphne. He brought her supplies that Amelia did not comprehend, but Daphne knew their use. She said, in fact, that Sir Richard was obviously quite knowledgeable about gardening and farming.

"He tells me about the crops and animals on his estate," Daphne said. "He must oversee much of the work himself."

"He did once mention his interest in pigs," Amelia recalled.

Daphne laughed. "Pigs are his passion!"

"Then he told you of them?"

"He told me his sow was the largest and most beautiful this side of London."

Daphne did not seem surprised by the description, but Amelia could not quite imagine a sow that could be described as beautiful. Still, she could not help but be pleased by Sir Richard's interest in Daphne's garden. In some way his interest, which could be seen by all the neighbors who peered out from behind their curtains to Amelia's certain knowledge, for she had seen their curtains move, added respectability to her young sister's unusual pastime. He would stand on the path and point out areas, exclaiming with Daphne over such features as shade and proper drainage. He noticed, before Amelia, the first green tips of new plants that broke the earth.

When he came to retrieve Lady Isabelle in the early afternoon, he would insist on having Daphne and Clarisse or Berdine join him in the carriage so that he could take them round the shops. Although he always asked Amelia, she declined. She did not wish to spend more time in his company than need be for the most uncomfortable of reasons. She found that his nearness had some strange effect on her circulation, drawing the blood to her cheeks and causing her fingertips to go cold and tingly. She did not like these sensations at all.

To her relief he only brought the carriage occasionally, usually sending it with a maid to pick up Lady Isabelle.

"Still," she told herself, "it is desirable for him to take Berdine and Clarisse to the shops. Perhaps as their acquaintance strengthens, an attraction will form. It is possible that I have misjudged. With guidance he might be a suitable husband for one of them, after all."

At that point she was assuming that his interest in gaming was overstated by the gossips and that if this were so, no doubt the tales of women were also false. Perhaps, unknown to them all, the marchioness was a relative. That would explain his interest in her child. Perhaps they both stayed with him for reasons of health, an explanation that Amelia found herself favoring. After all, everyone knew of Scotland's damp weather. If the child had been sickly, what would be more natural than for her mother to whisk her off to the sunnier English climate of a cousin's estate?

The only problem with that explanation was that if there was ever an eight-year-old child who looked as though she had never sneezed in her life, it was the plump, pink-cheeked, lively little Lady Isabelle. It was all Amelia could do to keep the child seated long enough to give her the barest sort of instruction.

"Lady Isabelle," Amelia would say, "please resume your place so that we may once again recite the verb conjugation."

"I don't care to conjugate," Isabelle would pout from under her table, where she was on her hands and knees.

"Very well, Lady Isabelle, if you prefer, we shall recite proper nouns."

"I don't care to recite proper nouns," she replied, rolling over on her back and sticking her chubby legs in the air so that her feet pressed on the underside of the table and made it wobble.

"Lady Isabelle!" Amelia exclaimed, exasperated. "I must insist that you come out from under the table. Your mother would be most displeased."

"My mother is always displeased," Isabelle said. Crawling out, she stood and hopped around the room, to the wide-eyed delight of the Tupper girls.

If such behavior continued, it would be reported in all the homes in Puddleafton, thoroughly undermining whatever reputation Amelia had managed to procure for her school. Taking the child by the hand, she led her into the entryway and closed the door to the classroom.

"Now, my dear," she said, hoping to sound kind but firm, "your mother has especially requested that we concentrate on your pronunciation of the French language. That is why Sir Richard brings you here every day. Surely you do not wish to disappoint the very people who most care for you?"

"I don't care for French," Isabelle said, shaking her head so hard that her red curls bobbed about.

"I know it seems difficult, but it has great charm," Amelia said weakly.

"It is not difficult, it is dull!"

"Is there something you would prefer to learn?" Amelia asked.

"No," said Isabelle. "I do not like to learn."

"Then what do you wish to do?"

The child tilted her head and gave Amelia a teasing glance, as though to test her. "What I wish," she said slowly, her plump rosy mouth carefully forming the words, "is to study with Miss Daphne's group. They do not have to stay in their chairs and they sing songs and go for walks outdoors."

"But Miss Daphne instructs the younger girls," Amelia said. "You are much too old and you know your sums and letters."

The young lady stamped her foot. "That is what I wish!"

Amelia thought quickly, knowing that she must both control the child and keep her as a student, yet also aware that she could not discipline her with a sharp look as she could the other girls. The child was much too spoiled. Finally she said, "I think Miss Daphne might consider allowing you in her class if you were to prove of use to her, Lady Isabelle."

"In what form would that be?" the child asked.

"I think you could teach the smaller girls some poems in French, which would be most useful, but it would mean that you would have to learn them first from me and be able to pronounce all the words to perfection."

Lady Isabelle hesitated, then said, "Would I be allowed to go out of doors with Miss Daphne, then?"

Amelia nodded.

The child sighed, then said, "I shall do it, Miss Grant."

"Then come along now and we shall go over a poem," Amelia said, leading the way back into the schoolroom.

Behind her she heard Lady Isabelle say, "I shall do it, but I do believe you are using me quite badly."

Amelia was glad she had her back to the girl so that Isabelle could not see Amelia smile.

Daphne found the plan acceptable. "The younger girls are so in awe of her, I think it will be helpful," she admitted. "I shall tell them that she will join us each day as soon as they have completed their reading lesson. It should be an inspiration."

And it was. The smaller children bent over their slates with renewed enthusiasm, so that an unusual hush fell in the dining room and their reading and writing skills rapidly improved, while in the classroom a temporarily subdued Lady Isabelle pushed her round little mouth into the shapes required to properly pronounce the words of the short poem that Amelia taught her.

Afterwards Daphne took Lady Isabelle and the younger girls into the kitchen garden where they sat on the bench, or hopped around it, and recited aloud their new French lesson with their arms flapping in rhythm. It was a method of teaching that Amelia could not imagine being condoned by any of the learned authorities on the education of the young, but perhaps none of them had ever had a Lady Isabelle cast into their schoolroom.

Two weeks and four poems later Sir Richard himself stopped at the door to speak with Amelia after Lady Isabelle had darted past in search of Daphne.

"I am quite impressed, Miss Grant, with the poetry our young student recites to me in the carriage. I am no authority on pronunciation, certainly, having never mastered the language, but I do understand French well enough and can sort a proper accent from the lame likes of mine."

"How kind of you to mention it," Amelia said.

"My mentioning is meant as a sincere compliment, but it also is a means to lead to a question."

"Ah! And what is that, Sir Richard?"

"Our little lady tells me she is not a mere student now, but is also a teacher."

Once again Amelia felt blood flow to her cheeks, setting her face and throat afire and making her appear, she feared, like some silly child. She explained how it had come about that Isabelle taught poems to Daphne's girls, hoping that the quaver she felt in her voice could not be heard. He would think she had no more presence than a milkmaid.

"I have always thought you extraordinary," he said. "Yet you continue to exceed my expectations."

She darted a look at him. Was he making fun of her? "If you do not consider it suitable for Lady Isabelle to instruct the other children, I shall, of course, arrange otherwise."

"Not suitable!" he exclaimed. "Indeed, dear Miss

Grant, to my certain knowledge, no one has ever succeeded in causing Isabelle to do anything other than exactly what she wishes. I believe you have done the impossible, and, between the two of us, I think it is a greater accomplishment in her education than any amount of French grammar might ever be."

"Oh! I am relieved. I feared otherwise."

"Did you think you were the only person who had ever been incapable of controlling the child? In that case I shall not tell you how many governesses and personal maids that little lady has managed to cause to resign in her eight years. The information would give you far too much confidence and I find you charming exactly as you are."

"Now you do tease me!" Amelia cried, then clamped her mouth shut lest she say something further that she had not meant to say.

He laughed and the fine lines she found so becoming wreathed his face. "I thought you would never notice, my dear. Good day."

He bobbed a quick bow and hurried to the carriage, leaving Amelia in the doorway, her heart pounding, her mind awhirl, as she could not understand why he wished her to think he teased. An undertone existed in his conversation, and she knew it, but as all her relationships with males had been extremely formal, she also knew that any lapses into informality were quite beyond her comprehension.

CHAPTER 10

The village of Puddleafton, Amelia discovered, was built not so much around the common that her house faced, as around a tree. This information came from Sir Richard, who often proved to be the source of a fascinating variety of facts. He also proved to be a source of mystery and intrigue, as well as temptation, showing up on her doorstep with such constant offers to accompany her to the village that she found it more and more difficult to refuse.

"I do not need the carriage," she explained carefully, more than once. "It is but a pleasant walk to the shops, sir, and we are well capable of carrying home our purchases. The shops deliver any larger items."

Finally, in exasperation, he said, "If you will not let me do you the favor of providing you with transportation, Miss Grant, would you be so kind as to do me the favor of providing me with companionship on a stroll through the village?"

"Oh," Amelia said softly, unable to think of anything else to say.

"Oh, indeed," he said. "And you cannot complain that we are unchaperoned. The whole village will be watching us and will carefully guard your reputation."

"It is not my reputation that worries me," Amelia said.

"What is it, then?"

"I fear that I impose on you. Your friendship with my aunt should not require you to fortfeit your valuable time in constant worry about the Grant household."

He muttered an oath under his breath that Amelia pretended not to hear, as she was not sure of its meaning. She was, however, sure that she did not want to hear it repeated. And so she had quickly grabbed her bonnet and pelisse and hurried out with him toward the shops, leaving Berdine to handle the afternoon lessons. Why he had arrived an hour early to collect Lady Isabelle was still unclear, but Amelia decided not to question him, as his answers today were vague. The whole comment about her reputation was so ridiculous as to deserve to be ignored. It was hardly as though they were wandering in the moonlight. A stroll through the shops at midday with the whole village watching from behind their slightly stirring curtains could not be mistaken for anything other than a courtesy call, especially as the village was well informed of the friendship between Sir Richard and the Misses Grants' aunt.

As they left the common and turned off the bridge onto the high road, Sir Richard said, "Perceive the tree across the way, Miss Grant."

"I often have," she said. "It seems a bit in the way of the road."

"Proving my point exactly that you need guidance through Puddleafton," Sir Richard said. "Only a stranger would think that the tree interfered with the road. The reverse is true. That oak has been in that spot for over a hundred years, planted by an early Wyland to corner-mark his land boundaries. The road is a newcomer, laid here in the past fifty years. Many a driver has complained about the tree. As coaches become larger, the road's curve is difficult to maneuver. But the town of Puddleafton is adamant. Those who do not revere their tree need not use their road."

The oak twisted its heavy old limbs in spirals, spreading out to a width greater than its height, and a rock wall had been built around the spreading limbs to protect them. The wall was the height of a bench, forming a resting place in the road's turn for both the tree boughs and strollers who cared to sit on it. An old man leaned there now, his face turned to the sun, sucking on his pipe. He nodded when they passed.

Sir Richard said, "Good afternoon, Jacob."

"Good day to you, sir. And you, ma'am."

Amelia felt the old man's eyes following them. Sir Richard explained, "His father served my grandfather, but old Jacob went to Cornwall to make his fortune in the mines. He came back poorer than he left, but luckier than most. Many did not even return with their lives."

"Do you know everyone in the village?"

"Most of them," he said. "My mother knew the name of every newborn child, but I cannot claim such distinction, though I try to remember."

"That's kind of you," Amelia said.

"Kind? In my mother it was probably a kindness. With me it is more an obligation. Do you see the gray stone used for the shop row? Came from those hills. But the paler stones, those with the yellow tinge, notice if you will in the second house beyond the shops, that's from the old walls built by the Romans."

Startled, Amelia said, "Do you mean the owner tore down an historic wall?"

"You are interested in history, then?" he asked.

"I find it fascinating."

"I must plan a tour of the historic sites for you," he said.

"I shouldn't want you to be so put by for time," she said.

"I could bring my son," he said. "He has not seen the sites and it is time he did. Perhaps Daphne would accompany us also, making it an educational outing."

Amelia tilted her head to peer past her bonnet's rim up into his face. "I should like to meet your son," she said, meaning it. As Sir Richard had never before mentioned the boy, she had not known if it were proper for her to do so, even though Aunt Sophie had told her of him. She feared it would sound as though she were prying into his private life which, of course, she was not. She had no interest in his private life unless he decided to court one of her sisters. Then she would have reason to pry. Meanwhile, it should cast some light on his character if she could meet his son.

"Thomas is a good lad," he said.

"I am sure he must be," she said. She did not doubt the child's quality. However, if he seemed well cared for and educated, that would reflect some light on Sir Richard's quality, would it not? As soon as the thought crossed her mind, Amelia thought of her own father and realized that the connection between parent and child often bespoke nothing revealing to the outsider. She and her sisters were what they were due to the devotion of their mother, not as a result of her father's failure.

"As for the wall," Sir Richard said, opening the door to the notions shop, "the Romans did an excellent job of rock trimming. The stones are well squared and easy to restack, which makes them desirable. I do not think householders have demolished the wall. Rather, in many places it has fallen down and they have carted away the loose stones."

"Are there parts of the wall near here? I thought it was much farther north."

"It is. But some of its stones have been carted long distances. I doubt that anyone who does not live here knows that bits of the Roman wall now reside in Puddleafton."

The shopkeeper appeared from behind a curtained doorway, saying, "Good day, Sir Richard. Ah, Miss Grant! Good day, m'am," and pulled a chair out from the table that filled the shop's center. Amelia returned his greeting and sat down. Sir Richard called the shopkeeper by name.

"I am looking for a rather smallish bodkin," Amelia said.

The shopkeeper lifted a round-topped chest from the row of shelves that lined the shop's walls and carried it to the table. "I have a fine assortment, both bone and ivory, Miss Grant."

After he'd lifted the lid and removed a small inner tray of larger bodkins, Amelia poked through a layer of narrower bodkins. Since the return of Clarisse from her unfortunate journey, the tatting had renewed, but something in Clarisse's unhappy mind caused her fingers to do finer and finer work so that she had managed camisole trims so delicate that a proper ribbon could not be drawn through them. Berdine and Amelia had decided that, rather than upset Clarisse by pointing out this problem, they would draw a linen thread through the trimming to form the gathering at the waist. Unfortunately, none of their bodkins was small enough to pass through the tatting, and the thread was too large for the eyes of their needles.

"This should suit," Amelia said, picking the smallest bodkin in the chest.

"Very good, Miss Grant," the man said. He disappeared with the bodkin, hurrying behind the curtain, then returned with it in a twist of cloth scrap. Amelia slipped it into her reticule, pressed a penny into the shopkeeper's hand, then left with Sir Richard.

"If you would buy something of a greater size, I would be able to carry it for you, thereby justifying my presence," Sir Richard said. "I feel foolish about offering to carry what must be the smallest bodkin in Puddleafton."

Amelia laughed. "I do detect the scent of gingerbread from the baker's shop. Perhaps I should buy a cake. Daphne is especially fond of it."

"I am myself. But if I should take home a gingerbread cake from the baker, my own baker would quit his position on the spot."

"Fortunately, I need have no such worry about Dora. She has far too much to do to also handle the baking."

"Then gingerbread it is," he said, turning in to the

baker's. Before Amelia could protest, he had picked a much larger cake than she could afford, paid for it, and taken the warm cake, folded in a bleached cloth, to carry home.

When they were on the road, Amelia said, "I should have brought my basket."

"Then I would have been of no use," Sir Richard said.

"Yes, but you see, the baker has had to use his own toweling to wrap the cake."

His eyebrows rose. His light eyes widened in surprise. "What else would he use?"

"Why, we bring our own tea towel to the bakery," Amelia said. "But it matters not. Daphne will return this one tomorrow."

They had reached the bridge. Sir Richard stopped, swinging in front of her so that Amelia stopped also and was forced to gaze up at him. His face was solemn, his mouth serious, but the lines crinkling around his eyes betrayed his amusement. "Miss Amelia Grant, I have thoroughly misjudged. I had thought it was I who would teach you about the village. My knowledge is superficial, I do believe. I have, in weak moments, purchased sweets from the bakery, and always they were wrapped thus. Yet no one asked that I return the cloth."

"They would not of you," Amelia said.

"Yet I should have guessed."

"No doubt you overpaid them well past the value of the cloth," she said.

"Possibly. Still, it does occur to me that my knowledge is confined to my own background."

"Is it not for all of us?"

"Umm. You may be right. Indeed, I suppose you

are. You are an extremely introspective female." He resumed walking toward her cottage, and Amelia, fearing they were a bit late and wishing to return before the children were dismissed, hurried her steps.

At her doorway she invited him into the entry, then said, "Wait while I fetch Lady Isabelle."

"Am I to have carried this cake with its marvelous aroma, only to be sent away without a taste?" he asked.

Shocked at her own oversight, Amelia said, "My, no! I do apologize. Please, would you care to stay for tea with my sisters and Lady Isabelle?"

"I would, indeed, care to do just that, and you can have no idea of the gratification I receive from having my obvious and ill-mannered hint so quickly and graciously acted upon."

Amelia chewed her lip, a slight frown creasing her forehead, while she tried to determine what to do with Sir Richard now that he had accepted. Slowly she said, "If I take you through the schoolroom, I fear the children will be much too excited to keep their thoughts on their lessons. Yet I hesitate to ask you to remain in the hallway. Ah, I shall not let this be a problem, Sir Richard. Come along, the children are very nearly through with their day's work."

"No, please," he said, touching her arm to stop her as she turned toward the schoolroom door. "I shall slip out the front and around the house and go through the kitchen door."

Amelia's violet-blue eyes widened in dismay. "You cannot do that!"

"I can and shall," he said. "And I give you me word as a gent that I'll mind me manners and not pinch the kitchen maid!"

"Pinch the—! Oh! I would never—!" Amelia stopped, unable to think of another word of reply, and stared, open mouthed, while color rushed to her cheeks.

Sir Richard was already out the door, but he leaned back around it, peered into her face, said solemnly, "I know that such a thought would not be permitted to cross your mind. How could I have suggested it?" and disappeared around the house.

Amelia stamped her foot in agitation. Really! When she left Pickerton Cross she had believed that she'd left behind irritating males. She could not remember stamping her foot or feeling such absolute fury since her last encounter with her father about the money box. If there had been any object near at hand to throw, she would have thrown it, but there was little satisfaction to be gained from throwing her bonnet or cape, as they would land with such insignificant plops.

Despite his wealth and title and friendship with Aunt Sophie, it did appear that Sir Richard would be a most unsatisfactory match for Berdine or Clarisse. If he were to marry either, Amelia would be forced to accept him as a member of the family, and such an irritation was not to be borne.

As soon as she thought it, she stamped her foot again. However impossible he might be, he could provide security to either sister, which was more than any of them had ever had. She must not discourage him.

Amelia returned through the schoolroom to the dining room, nodding to Berdine as she passed her desk. The children were bent over their books. Blond Anne Measure was not at her place but Amelia saw the tips of her slippers protruding from around the door. Berdine picked up the small copper bell and rang it.

"Young ladies," she said softly, "kindly replace your books and slates."

Amelia went into the dining room, glanced out the window, and saw Daphne on the side path with the smaller children. Sir Richard had stopped to talk to them. They gathered close to him; their plump hands pressed to their mouths to hold back their giggles. What could he be saying to them, she wondered. As she watched him smiling and bending toward them, looking so tall and trim and handsome with his brown hair gleaming in the sun, she felt quite annoyed. He had no right to look so proper and behave so—so—"Oh, my," she whispered, "I really do not know how to describe his behavior. He never does anything that is truly improper and yet—oh, dear."

He moved toward the garden door while Daphne pushed the children toward the front door. Amelia heard his steps across the pantry, heard Dora exclaim, "Sir Richard!"

"Think of me as the baker delivering the gingerbread," he said, his low voice carrying through the room.

"I never! I must say!"

"It did seem I would least disturb the schoolroom if I came through this way," he explained. "I have been invited to remain for tea."

"Have you, now!" Dora gasped. "Oh, I do—forgive me, sir, that is, would you be wanting to go on through to the dining room?"

This is more than I can bear, Amelia decided, and returned to the schoolroom before Sir Richard offered to help Dora serve the tea, an offer that would not have surprised Amelia, although it would have offended her sense of propriety. Berdine had already dismissed the girls. She and Daphne were busy tying bonnet strings and buttoning capes.

Berdine said, "Lady Isabelle is ready."

"Lady Isabelle is to stay to tea with us," Amelia said.

Lady Isabelle pulled off her bonnet and shook out her red curls. "Will you have muffins with currants?" she asked.

"We will have a gingerbread," Amelia said.

"I like that! We *never* have gingerbread," she exclaimed.

"Sir Richard will stay, also," Amelia said.

Berdine glanced at Daphne, who shrugged. Berdine said, "Amelia, I hope it will not inconvenience you, dear, but you see, that is—" A blush rose in her throat and she stopped.

"What is it?" Amelia asked.

Berdine turned a pleading look toward Daphne, her small face pinched with worry.

"It is only that Berdine and I were asked to tea at the parish house," said Daphne. "We had thought to walk home with Anne. But is it such a worry, Berdine? I should think you could go with Anne and I could remain here to take tea with Sir Richard."

"I could not go alone!" Berdine stammered.

"Don't be a muttonhead," Daphne said.

Amelia noticed the round, upturned faces of the children, all waiting in the doorway, listening eagerly. Hoping to keep her voice soft and unemotional, she said, "But of course you must go along if you were invited, Daphne. Clarisse will be at table."

Daphne leaned toward her and, cupping her hand, whispered in Amelia's ear, "Clarisse is in her room having another of her crying spells."

Now Amelia truly wished she had something she could throw, possibly something heavy and, better yet, directly at Sir Richard. In all fairness she knew that he could not be responsible for invitations from the parish house or for Clarisse's tears, but at the moment she did not feel the least interest in being fair. Her voice flat, she forced a smile and said, "That will be quite satisfactory, Daphne. Do you go along now. Good afternoon, young ladies. Come with me, Lady Isabelle."

As she marched to the tea table with Isabelle at her heels, she thought of a confusion of explanations to give Sir Richard, but when he walked in from the kitchen carrying the serving tray, followed by Dora with the gingerbread neatly sliced on a porcelain plate, her mind went blank. She could only manage a weak thank you.

Isabelle scrambled up onto a chair, her whole face curling into smiles and dimples at the sight of the gingerbread. "Nurse gives me very boring bread and hardly ever jam."

"I was not told!" Sir Richard exclaimed, as he arranged the tray in front of Amelia. "You should have said such to me, Isabelle. Of course you may have jam."

"Please do have a chair," Amelia said weakly, unused to having a man arrange a tea tray for her convenience. When he had sat down, she poured the tea.

"Have you gingerbread cakes, Sir Richard?" Isabelle asked. "No one has ever brought any to me."

121

"On that point you are no more neglected than I am, my dear. Gingerbread is one of those items that do not come out of my kitchens."

"Could you not order it?" the child demanded.

"I could not! I am in terror of my kitchen servants. Ask me to speak firmly to the grooms or coachmen, dear Isabelle, or even to your nurse, which, by the way, I shall about this matter of jam. But please do not require me to speak to the kitchen."

"Then I shall speak to them," said Lady Isabelle. "I think that gingerbread cake is a fine idea."

"If they all turn in their notices and we are left with nothing but dry bread and water, I hope you will not be unhappy," Sir Richard said solemnly.

"It would appear to me that you do not know how to handle your kitchen," the child said, matching his solemn tone. "You must ask my mother to do it. I am sure she handles our servants very well."

"I am sure she does," Sir Richard said, a bit more emphatically than Amelia would have expected one to speak of a guest.

Turning to Amelia, Isabelle said, "You must handle your servants very well, Miss Grant. You get gingerbread. Do you also get jam?"

Amelia laughed, relieved at the ease that the child's presence brought to a situation she had thought might be awkward. If Berdine and Clarisse could not be at the table to impress Sir Richard with their beauty or charm, at least it would do well to impress him with the pleasantness of the household. "I have but Dora to handle and Dora is so well trained that I need seldom give her orders."

"There, you see! That is it, Sir Richard! You must better train your servants. Perhaps Miss Grant could teach you how to do it. She is a very good teacher, you know. Ever so much nicer than my governess."

His eyes twinkled. "I do not think that Miss Grant would accept me as a student, Isabelle."

"Oh. I quite forgot. She only teaches girls," Isabelle said, then filled her mouth with gingerbread.

As Amelia passed the cake to Sir Richard, she said, "I think I should have something else to offer you. It does seem to me that gentlemen prefer wine to tea, but I must admit that I know nothing of wines and so have none to offer. Or am I mistaken? Is it something other than wine?"

"Some take a glass of sherry," he said. "I rather prefer tea."

Amelia nodded and hoped her relief did not show on her face. It was good to know that he was not a man who needed spirits at midafternoon. She had heard of men who always required liquor, even upon rising, and she was sure that they did not make good husbands for such gentle girls as her sisters.

Just when Amelia had managed to relax, the door opened and Clarisse entered.

"Oh," she said, "I did not know you were here, Sir Richard."

He stood and reached out a hand to motion her to a chair. "Miss Clarisse. How pleasant—my dear, have you had ill news?"

He, like Amelia, had noticed at once the reddened eyes and the letter, crumpled in the tightened fist.

"N-n-no," Clarisse whispered, then wailed, "it is much, much worse than that!"

CHAPTER 11

Sir Richard leaped up, tipping over his chair. As it crashed to the floor, he managed to catch Clarisse, who appeared about to faint dead away. If it were me, Amelia thought wryly, I should simply crash over like the chair. Still, it was well that even in fainting, Clarisse remained something of a wax doll, her face paling to a perfection of ladylike beauty, her slim hands fluttering gracefully, her slender form swaying like a flower stalk. The tear-stained letter dropped from her grasp.

Isabelle jumped down from her chair and caught it up. Amelia said, "Isabelle," with schoolroom firmness and held out her hand.

The child handed her the letter. More gently, Amelia said, "Thank you, Lady Isabelle. Come have another piece of gingerbread, dear."

Sir Richard had managed to place Clarisse in a chair, where she remained upright, though still entrancingly pale. Before Amelia could ring for Dora, he had picked up an extra cup from the tray, filled it with tea, and pressed it into Clarisse's hands. Worse, he lifted it to her lips as though she were an invalid. The whole scene bore a sense of familiarity that Amelia could not think proper. It was best, she decided, that Berdine was at the parish house. She would not have approved of Sir Richard's arm around Clarisse's shoulders.

A memory stirred in Amelia's mind through the worried thoughts. Had he not bent over her once? Ah. It was in Bath at Aunt Sophie's house when she had choked on a bite of food.

Under other circumstances Amelia would have rushed to Clarisse and begged her tell of her cause for such sorrow, but she was all too aware of Isabelle's fascination with the scene. Above her full and chewing little mouth, Isabelle's eyes watched avidly.

Slipping the letter beneath the tea tray, Amelia said, "Clarisse has been unwell lately. Dearest, I think you have come downstairs too soon. You should have called for Dora to help you."

Sir Richard, following Amelia's glance at Isabelle, said, "Indeed, Miss Clarisse, it never does to rise too quickly from sickbed. These springtime chills do leave one lightheaded."

Talking through her mouthful of gingerbread, Isabelle said, "I think she got a wicked letter."

"A young lady never speaks until her mouth is empty," Amelia said.

"I—I am better now, thank you," Clarisse said, sitting forward. Sir Richard set her cup on the table and withdrew his arm.

"May I guess that you have eaten nothing today?" he said. "That will not do, my dear. One must feed these chills or they quickly turn to fever." Pushing open the kitchen door, he said, "Dora, Miss Clarisse has arrived down for tea. Bring her something more substantial. Have you any cheese?"

"You speak firmly enough to Miss Grant's

kitchenmaid," Isabelle said. "Why cannot you do so with your own?"

"Dora is a very superior person," Sir Richard said. He closed the door and leaned over the child's shoulder. "My own cooks have not her superior temperament. However, if you will cease to pummel me on the subject, Isabelle, I promise by my honor to have jam on your tray."

Isabelle giggled. Clarisse watched, bewildered. When Dora appeared with a tray of cheese and biscuits, Clarisse could only gaze at them through misty eyes. Sir Richard insisted that she eat, claiming nothing else would revive her spirits, thus forcing Clarisse to either argue or resort to her usual table practice. As Clarisse could not speak without breaking into sobs, she did what Amelia had known she would do. She crumbled the biscuits slowly into bits and nibbled tiny bites from the cheese.

Sir Richard said kindly, "If you have quite finished, Isabelle, I do think we must be hurrying home. Your mother will think us lost."

"She may think you lost, but she will not miss me," Lady Isabelle said, licking the last crumbs from her fingers.

"Either way, I think we must thank Miss Grant for her hospitality."

He made his bows and took the child's hand to lead her from the room, for it seemed unlikely she would withdraw of her own choice. As Amelia accompanied them to the door and arranged Isabelle's bonnet strings, Sir Richard said, "If there is ought I can do for your sister, Miss Grant, I hope you will call on me. I could send along my physician."

"No, thank you, I think she will soon be better."

"Yes, so do I."

"She is not ill," Isabelle said clearly. "She has had a wicked message. I think someone has written her of a terrible murder."

Sir Richard bent over the child, his face set firmly, opened his mouth with the obvious intent of rebuking her, then turned away and hurried out of the house. Amelia saw his shoulders shaking.

Amelia tucked a stray red curl under the lace-edged bonnet. "Lady Isabelle, I cannot let your imagination mislead you. You did, of course, see a letter and you are quite correct. That is no doubt what has upset Miss Clarisse. But the message is probably of an elderly relative who is gravely ill. It is *not* of a murder."

Isabelle thought, her face serious, then said, "You have not read the letter yet, Miss Grant. When you read it, will you tell me truly if it is a wicked letter?"

"One does not speak of the contents of a letter sent to another person. Oh, very well. I shall promise this much. If the letter contains news of a murder, Lady Isabelle, I shall certainly tell you."

"Do not forget that you have *promised,*" Isabelle said, and hurried out after Sir Richard.

When Amelia joined Clarisse, her sister was sitting with her elbows on the table, gazing unseeing out the window, tears glimmering on her lashes. She could say nothing without causing her voice to break. Amelia waited while Clarisse slowly sipped her cup of tea. Then she handed back the letter and suggested that whatever it was, Clarisse put it out of sight unless she wished everyone in Puddleafton to know its content.

Clarisse said slowly, "Not everyone, Amelia, but I must tell someone, and I think it must be you."

Amelia suspected that she did not want to know the content, but she nodded.

"It is from Edmond, my poor Edmond," Clarisse said. "He—he writes that—that we shall never meet again." Her voice broke. Amelia waited while Clarisse sipped more tea, then watched patiently as Clarisse's long fingers crumbled the biscuit bits into nothing.

"I—Amelia, he says that he understands that—that we are of a different kind. That is not so, Amelia! He is as fine as we, is he not? Yet it is because I was companion to Lady Ethelwynne, and now he knows that I am related to the baronet, yet I see not what that matters. We may be descended from landed gentry, Amelia, and dear Edmond from shopkeepers, as Aunt Sophie pointed out to me—"

"Did she?" Amelia had to interrupt.

"She did, and she said it was quite impossible for a Stafford to marry a shopkeeper."

"I think that rather overstates the case," Amelia said, "but the truth is that with Aunt Sophie's social connections and your beauty, even the lack of a marriage settlement, need not prevent you from making a more suitable marriage, Clarisse. And I rather think that Aunt Sophie might arrange some sort of settlement if you were to marry well."

Clarisse wailed, "What does that mean, marry well?"

"To a title, my dear, or to a fortune. A fortune would be better, as it would offer security. It is something we Grants have not had."

"But Edmond is not penniless."

"Has he offered for you, then?"

"How could he do that when he knows—when Lady Ethelwynne stood right there in the garden and told him that he must never see me or speak to me again, that he was quite out of his sphere. That is what she said, out of his sphere."

Amelia sighed. "I cannot think what to tell you, Clarisse. I can only point out that a gentleman of inheritance has an income that outlives him and continues to provide for his widow and children, while the income of a shopkeeper, though it may be quite adequate, tends to die with the shopkeeper. I have known many a penniless widow, Clarisse, and it is not a position I would wish on you."

"I do not see how we can be so particular when we are penniless ourselves," Clarisse moaned.

"Ah, but that is why we must be particular. There, Clarisse, please do not cry. I think your Mr. Chicore must think the same, which is why he has written you his farewell. I daresay he has your concern at heart, knowing that with your connections, you have good expectations. He is wise and kind to decide not to stand in your way."

Clarisse sniffed, searched her sleeves for her handkerchief, found one that was more lace trim than linen square, and managed to wipe away her tears. "Please, Amelia, what are my expectations?"

"Aunt Sophie believes that you were too young and inexperienced when first we visited Bath. She wishes you to stay home for another six months and help with the school. During the summer she will be at her country home and she will hold a few small parties, nothing so grand as the balls at Bath. We shall all attend. It will be an opportunity for you and

129

Berdine to observe the manners of Aunt Sophie's friends and to join their conversations. Conversation seems especially important, Clarisse. Young women are supposed to say clever things.''

"Clever things?" Clarisse rubbed at her reddened eyes. "What do you mean, clever things?"

"Wit. Quick reply. Oh, it is hard to explain, but Aunt Sophie thinks that if you are exposed to small groups of the *ton*, you will soon adopt their manners."

"Clever things. I do not understand."

"It matters not. You are prettier than most. The gentlemen find you charming. Perhaps as you become more accustomed to their company, you will speak with greater ease, and I think this matter of wit is overdone." Amelia spoke more to herself than to Clarisse, mulling through her thoughts, aware that she herself had no gift for empty phrases that were meant to allure and mystify the gentlemen. In her own case it did not matter, as she did not seek to attract anyone, but in Clarisse's case she suspected that her lack of wit could be overlooked in favor of her beauty if she could be taught simple, pleasant conversation.

Clarisse said slowly, "Even if one of Aunt Sophie's gentlemen offered for me, I could not accept him."

"What? How can you know? He might be very charming. Clarisse, suppose Sir Richard offered for you."

"Sir Richard? Sir Richard?" Clarisse blinked. "I could not marry Sir Richard."

"But why not?" demanded Amelia. While part of her mind was staggered at the thought of anyone rejecting Sir Richard, another part had odd sensations of relief that she could not comprehend. "He is a fine gentleman and I think he would make a generous and suitable husband."

"Perhaps. But, he is too old for me."

"Old! He is not so very old! I should think he is barely past thirty," Amelia exclaimed.

"That is old!" Clarisse cried, then added softly, "It is not his age, Amelia. And I do like him. He is very kind. But—but—Amelia, I cannot marry someone else when I *love* Edmond!"

"Oh, Clarisse. He has made his parting. I fear you must forget him."

"He may forget *me,*" Clarisse wailed, "but I shall never cease to love *him*!" Grabbing her handkerchief and letter, she fled from the room. Amelia heard Clarisse's slippers tap rapidly up the stairs.

The situation with Clarisse was becoming more than Amelia knew how to manage, she decided, as she wandered into the schoolroom and methodically straightened the chairs and tables and stacked the slates. Perhaps it would be wise to write to Aunt Sophie to discern whether her aunt had yet forgiven Clarisse's behavior. In that context Amelia could only hope that the fine and disdainful Lady Ethelwynne, who obviously lacked any sort of compassion, was not too dear a friend of Aunt Sophie's. Had the lady a whit of Christian charity, she would have realized that Clarisse was young, inexperienced, foolish, and immature, but also very pure of heart and mind. It was beyond Clarisse's gentle nature to comprehend the impropriety of accepting words and gestures of affection from a man whom she considered acceptable. That he was not acceptable was obvious to Amelia. A man of character would not meet an unchaperoned young woman on someone else's property without announcement or invitation. But that a person of Clarisse's simple nature would fail to recognize such a shortcoming, was within reason. Therefore, this Lady Ethelwynne lacked reason. As Aunt Sophie was supremely reasonable, Amelia hoped that Aunt Sophie would by now have seen the situation in its true colors and forgiven Clarisse.

As for Clarisse, Amelia convinced herself that the child needed time and the right temptation to alter the attitude of her heart. If Sir Richard did not meet her fancy, odd as that might seem, then no doubt she would find the exceptionally handsome Lord Pendarvin more to her approval.

That thought settled comfortably in her mind, Amelia smiled at the schoolroom and decided that all she need do now was insure that Clarisse meet more people, converse more freely, and be often invited to the same parties as his lordship in the coming summer. Therein lay a purpose that Aunt Sophie could arrange. Yes. The next step would be a letter to Aunt Sophie.

But while letters might well solve turmoils, they also tended to introduce them.

Berdine and Daphne hurried in, their cheeks pink from the brisk air. Daphne pulled her cape from her shoulders, then handed Amelia a letter. "It was still on the entry table."

"I quite forgot to notice," Amelia said, studying her name on the envelope. "I wonder who might write to me. I do not know the script."

"Open it and look at the signature," Daphne said.

Unfolding the letter, Amelia read a name with

which she had no familiarity. With this lack of aid she returned to the beginning of the message.

"My dear Miss Grant," the letter said, "it has come to my attention that you may well be uninformed of your father's whereabouts. For this I must apologize, having presumed that he had corresponded with you earlier. It may also be true that my name is unknown to you. Therefore I must explain my relationship. Your father's uncle was married to my mother's cousin, and should that seem somewhat remote, let me hasten to add that as lads we lived within riding distance of each other and on occasion were tutored together. His interests were always close to my heart, yet the responsibilities of our adult years drew us to opposite corners of our country and for a period of time I found myself in India. Be that as it may, he has found his way to my home and I have been made young again with the renewal of our acquaintance. Indeed, the finding of a lost brother could give no greater joy.

"Let me assure you that he is well. He does, however, suffer some indisposition of temper and quite refuses to correspond with his family, a situation that occurs in many households, I am sure, and will with time correct itself. Meanwhile, be assured that he is cared for here and that any inquiry from you will be most gratefully answered by myself. Yours in faith and kinship, Henry Martin-Armsley."

"How peculiar!" Daphne said. "Where does this lost cousin reside?"

"I don't—ah—I see. I cannot say the name, Daphne. It is one of those long words with double consonants, but it is in the south of Wales."

"The south of Wales! I never! Did he ride all that way by public coach, do you think?"

"I cannot think how he came there. Mr. Martin-Armsley is quite unspecific."

"I think we must consider it a blessing that Father has found someone capable of his care," Berdine said.

Amelia added, "Far more blessing that he has managed to do so without returning to us a trail of debts."

"Is it not strange that Father did not write?" Berdine asked.

"I cannot recall him ever writing to anyone," Amelia said. "Still, I shall write both to him and to Mr. Martin-Armsley to thank him for his message and his care of Father. I have also a letter to write to Aunt Sophie. Perhaps I had best do so now." Amelia pulled open the desk drawer to search out her writing materials. "Was your tea at the parish house pleasant?"

She arranged the ink and paper, then realized she had had no reply. Glancing up, she saw Berdine and Daphne watching each other from their eyes' corners, as though unsure who should speak.

"Is it so difficult, then, to retell a teatime at the parish house?" Amelia asked.

"Oh, no, Amelia dear, it is only—it was pleasant. Most pleasant. There was nothing to tell—that is, one sips tea, that is rather all," Berdine finished weakly. "I—I must sort the linens. The laundress will be in tomorrow."

Was that a blush flaming Berdine's cheeks, or only

a bit of reflected windowlight? She turned and fled so quickly, and so unlike Berdine, that Amelia could not be sure.

To Daphne she said firmly, "Before you, too, disappear, young lady, I believe I would like a description of teatime at the parish house."

"A description, Amelia?"

"For a young lady who has no trouble relating all the village tattle, I should not consider that a challenge."

"It is not. Umm—the serving is done on a tea table in the parlor. Tea consisted of rock cake and cucumbers in the thinnest slices I have ever seen. There was no butter," Daphne said.

"And what is there in that to so confuse Berdine?"

Daphne tried to look solemn, but a thought turned up the corners of her mouth and her angel face looked a shade naughty. "I cannot think," she said smoothly. "Certainly there was nothing to confuse me."

"Daphne, you are being less than honest." A sudden thought caught Amelia. "Did you have tea with Berdine or did you slip off to the shops?"

"I did not!" Daphne said emphatically. "I had my tea at the parish house."

"I did not mean to imply—" Amelia paused, prepared to make an apology for her suspicions when a new suspicion arrived. "Daphne, I understand that you remained at the parish house, but with whom did you have tea?"

Daphne began to straighten again the chairs that Amelia had already straightened. She said lightly, "Oh, Amelia, you know how dull I find long conversations on religious topics, however much they may fascinate Berdine. Do you not, yourself?"

Amelia stood and stamped her foot. "Daphne! With whom did you have tea?"

Daphne arranged the candlesticks on the mantle, saying over her shoulder, "I had tea with Anne and the housekeeper. I suppose you may as well know. The housekeeper invites the gardener to join us in the kitchen." Turning, she said defiantly, "I cannot believe it is improper as long as she invites him and is there and pours herself. And he is ever so kind. He answers all my questions and knows all there is to know about the garden."

Amelia sank back into her desk chair and asked weakly, terrified of the answer, "How old is this gardener, Daphne?"

"How old?" Daphne's voice rose in honest surprise. "I'm sure I don't know! He looks one hundred, though he cannot be, but he's an odd, warty old man, bent over but stronger than he looks, and he knows everything."

Amelia let her breath out slowly. "I see. That's all right, then. But if you and Anne and the housekeeper are in the kitchen, where is Berdine?"

"She takes tea in the parlor with Mr. Measure," Daphne said, and, satisfied that she had relieved her sister's mind of worry about the propriety of taking tea with the gardener, Daphne skipped out of the room in search of her work boots.

Had she turned to look, she would have seen Amelia fold her arms on the desk and slowly lower her head into them, her shoulders sagging. As the Reverend John Measure was probably not much better off financially than the parish-house gardener, Amelia sincerely wished he were also old and warty. Or, if not that, then as far removed from Puddleafton as the questionable Mr. Edmond Chicore.

CHAPTER 12

April drifted into May. Daphne's garden flourished. Waves of bulbs pushed their green shoots through the sweet-smelling earth, spread their leaves, and spilled out their blossoms, until the front path resembled a stone bridgeway between the gently swaying tides of lavender, white, gold, and creamy yellows of narcissus and hyacinths and dillies. White petals floated like snowflakes from a plum tree in the common. The kitchen garden bragged straight rows of carrot tops and lettuce and leeks and neeps, while peavines wound themselves through the fence and beanrunners climbed their poles.

Dora scrubbed the windows and hung freshly laundered lace curtains. Berdine slit the seams of their old summer frocks, turned them inside out to the less faded side of the material, and restitched them. Clarisse embroidered cross- and featherstitching to hide the marks where Daphne's skirts had had their hems dropped.

Amelia paid all the shopkeepers and had enough left to buy dress lengths of new muslin for them all, as well as summer bonnets and new slippers.

And Mr. Martin-Armsley, like all good and unforeseen benefactors, kept their father in his care and away from their doorstep and money box.

Both the viscount and Sir Richard were frequent guests, stopping by most casually, which Amelia was not sure was quite the suitable decorum; yet she could not hold at-home hours, not being so graciously situated. As no one had yet turned out a volume of advice on the proper rules of entertaining for a household that required its members to earn their living and use their parlor for a schoolroom, she decided that she must not think on such worries. Instead, she did as best she could to show both gentlemen that her sisters had the quality required of a gentleman's wife, being pious, gentle, and accomplished in a variety of womanly skills.

Although she would have preferred to keep Daphne out of sight, as she in no way fit into this presentation of proper conduct, the two gentlemen concerned made that impossible. They constantly sought Daphne out.

"I suppose," Amelia said once to Berdine, "that they believe they must extend their courtesy and acceptance to the younger sister if they are to win the heart of the eligible sister. In the same way, then, do they lavish attention on me, no doubt as they would lavish it on the mother of an eligible."

Berdine bit off a thread and turned the sewing on her lap. "I am sure you are correct, Amelia. If either is to win the heart of our Clarisse, he must accept the rest of us as his relations. Still, one does wish Daphne were easier to accept."

Amelia did not bother to point out that the two gentlemen could not both choose Clarisse. And as she studied them more, she convinced herself that they would easily be swayed in the correct directions, with the viscount choosing Clarisse and whisking her off to his London home where she would shine beautifully as she acquired confidence. It was true that Clarisse's flair for wit had not developed as one might have hoped, but she had at least learned to keep her mouth formed into a shy smile. Was there not a place in the *ton* for a beautiful woman whose silence might be mistaken for mystery? Amelia decided that there must be.

As for Berdine, though she herself would deny it, being such a self-effacing little creature, Sir Richard was an excellent choice. If the tattle had some shred of truth and his life leaned toward gaming and had other undesirable aspects, Berdine's gentle faith would persuade him to better paths. And who better than Berdine to marry a widower and take over the task of loving care of his motherless child?

Then, if either husband could be imposed upon to accept Daphne into their households, and Amelia thought both showed a fond weakness for Daphne that promised well, Amelia could journey to Wales to discover her father's situation. By that time the good Mr. Martin-Armsley would have wearied of Father and Amelia could bring him back to Puddleafton. It was a better place for him than Pickerton Cross, as it was farther removed from gaming places.

For although Amelia was deeply grateful to have Father elsewhere at the moment, she had never intended to dodge permanently her responsibility to him.

If Miss Amelia Grant walked lightly through the lanes of Puddleafton, her market basket on her arm, her chin raised, and a dimpled smile on her face, it was because the sweet-scented springtime breezes matched her mood.

Or, as she had reason to think later, pride goeth before a fall.

As she hurried toward home, her new bonnet framing her face with pale blue ruching, her sprigged muslin stirring like flower petals in a breeze on her slender form, she saw the carriage with its emblem of the Marquess of Darmerdavin in front of her door. She nipped in, pulled free her bonnet, smoothed back her hair as best she could, took a deep breath, and entered the schoolroom. The marchioness confronted a nervous, red-faced Dora.

"Madam," Amelia said, "your daughter left more than an hour ago with a maid from Sir Richard's household."

"I have not come to find my daughter," the marchioness said. Her voice was sharp, and her face rigid, as though she were struggling to contain her temper.

Bewildered, Amelia said, "Then—then may I offer you tea? Do forgive me. Allow Dora to take your outer garments and then I must show you to the dining room to offer you a chair. I must apologize that we have not a parlor—"

"This is not a call," the marchioness said. "You may dismiss your maid. I only wish to speak with you, Miss Grant, and it can take but a moment to say what I must say."

Dora did not wait to be dismissed. She darted from the room to disappear into her kitchen and remain there well out of sight. If she pressed her ear to the door, it mattered not to Amelia, for she had no secrets from Dora. In such a small cottage, secrets would be impossible. As Dora had the discretion to pretend that she did not overhear, and the good sense not to repeat what she overheard, Amelia did not worry about her.

"Indeed, madam, I do hope there is no complaint as to Lady Isabelle's instruction," Amelia said.

"There is every complaint," the marchioness said. "Yet I shall not lower myself to discuss them with you. I was misled into believing you were qualified to teach my daughter, an error for which I must accept responsibility. I have come only to make it quite clear to you that I am withdrawing my daughter from your tutelage and that I must direct you nevermore to use my daughter's name in any form of reference in order to expand your enrollment."

Amelia paled but stood straight. "I have never so done."

The marchioness moved slightly toward her. Windowlight touched her face, showing clearly now the sharp, perfect features, the tight mouth, the pale skin, the edge of red hair beneath the silk-lined bonnet. "That is not quite as I have heard, but never mind. Those who have been misled into believing that the presence of Lady Isabelle in your school reflected on your quality, now are elsewise informed. Although I had no obligation to do so, I recognized that your connection with Miss Stafford, however fortunate it may be for you, was not of her doing. I, too, have carried the burden of undesired kinships, and therefore sympathize with her position. From such consideration I have made this call to inform you of Lady Isabelle's withdrawal and my own disapproval, presuming I must say no more of this matter."

As she could not guess the reason for the lady's obvious anger, and could not demand to be told it, all Amelia could say was, "Does Sir Richard know of this?"

"Sir Richard has gone to London. I am amazed that he did not so inform you himself," the marchioness said. "Good day, Miss Grant."

And before Amelia could say else, the marchioness swept past her, her silk gown rustling as though with disdain, and disappeared down the path and into her carriage.

At Amelia's elbow Dora said softly, "Best come have a cup of tea, miss. Pity we've nothing stronger to wash away the likes of her."

"Dora, I really do not—had she been here long?"

"Oh, no, miss, I only just heard her. That is, I did not hear her because I was at the garden door talking with Miss Daphne, if you understand, and I cannot all that well hear the door from the kitchen under any circumstances. But I think she must not have stood long, for her footman came round the back to find me. I ran right through to open the door."

"Dear me."

"Yes, miss. She pushed right past me into the room, demanding to see you. I tried to tell her, miss. Then I thought I should go call Miss Daphne, but she's all mud and work boots now, with her skirt caught up in her apron—"

"It's all right, Dora. It can't be changed. But did she say ought more of what she wanted?"

"No, miss."

Amelia carried her basket into the kitchen and set

it on the bare, scrubbed wood of the table. "It is quite beyond me, then. Sir Richard has commented favorably on Lady Isabelle's progress and certainly I have received no note or word from the marchioness. I cannot imagine what is wrong."

Dora shook her head, causing more wisps of taffy hair to fall loose from her frilled cap and frame her flushed face. She pursed her lips. Amelia could not guess if she closed her mouth against angry words or if she did that to stop from repeating what she knew.

Amelia could have asked Dora, but it would have put an edge to their relationship that might not be desirable. It would force Dora to admit that she overheard gossip. It would also force her to repeat what she might not wish to repeat. And it would dissolve the slight reserve that lay between them, making it awkward for Amelia to give Dora orders. Amelia was never overbearing or unkind with servants, but she knew from years of running her father's house that if she treated a servant as a sister, the servant would soon be giving orders to Amelia. Such an arrangement would be as uncomfortable for Dora as it would be for Amelia.

Instead, she hurried to the kitchen garden, seeking Daphne. The girl leaned on her rake handle, daydreaming, her blue eyes shining like bits of sky in her sun-browned face, her angel hair floating free of its ribbons. As ever, her bonnet hung unused down her back. Her skirt was caught up in her apron ribbons, tucked through so that it hung no lower than the apron and revealed a width of mud-spattered stockings above the boots.

"Ah, hullo, Amelia. You're back quickly. Come see my radishes. They're ready to pull."

144

"What were you thinking about just now?" Amelia asked.

"Now? Oh, that. I was thinking, it's not too late to turn up that bit of turf by the workshed and it catches the sun ever so. With a stretch of old net, I think I could cover the shed with a nice flowering vine."

"Did you see the footman come round the house?"

"Yes. He spoke to Dora. I think there was someone at the street door. Should I have gone round? I thought it best to leave Berdine to handle whoever it might be."

"Berdine is not within."

"Is she not? That's odd."

"Nor Clarisse."

"Ah, well, then I should guess they have walked over to the parish house. Do you think we might spare some old netting?"

"Netting? For the vine? Ask Dora. Perhaps there is something you could use in the boxroom." Amelia tightened a ribbon in her dark curls, chewed thoughtfully on her lower lip, then decided that if anyone might help her, it would be Daphne. Slowly she asked, "Daphne, have you heard talk of the marchioness being dissatisfied with Lady Isabelle's progress in our instruction?"

Daphne dug at a weed with her rake's edge. "I think she could not be. Lady Isabelle has learned quickly."

"That is not precisely what I asked."

"No." Daphne caught up the loosened weed in her muddy fingers and threw it on a pile at the row's end. "Everything else that I have heard is what you would call tattle, Amelia, and you would correct me if I were to repeat it."

"Circumstances vary the degrees of propriety," Amelia said, and hoped that this were so. "I think you had best tell me what you have heard."

"But it is untrue."

"Nevertheless."

"Very well, Amelia, but you will be displeased. I have not repeated what I felt did not warrant repeating."

"Daphne!" It was difficult to speak firmly, yet keep her voice below Dora's hearing. Worse, she could not even stamp her foot on the soft, quiet earth, as that would gain her nought but a shoeful of dirt.

"There has been a bit of tattle. I overheard some in the shops. It was foolish talk of Sir Richard's presence in the village with you and that it caused the marchioness some worry."

"But why should that be?"

"Some word she let drop, I presume."

"Daphne, I have quite enough trouble with the words and quizzings of others. From you I expect direct statements."

"But the statements were not direct! I but overheard bits." Daphne leaned her rake against the shed, wiped her hands on her apron, then finally met her sister's watchful eyes. "Very well. What they say is that the marchioness has dropped hints that she thinks Sir Richard comes to our house for reasons less than proper, that he has used her daughter as an excuse for his visits, and that in some way all this denotes that we are less than proper."

Amelia paled but said nothing.

Daphne hesitated, then continued, "It was so foolish I did not consider it worth mentioning to you, Amelia. I cannot think that anyone in the village would believe such a rumor. They repeat it to fill idle conversations. I would put it out of mind if I were you."

"Yet they repeat it! How could the lady say such things when she knows well enough that we rent our house from Sir Richard, that he is a friend of our aunt, and that he is never with any of us alone or other than in the daytime."

"I doubt that she mentions those facts. Then, also, she seems to have pointed out that our handsome viscount is a frequent caller."

"The viscount? But that is outrageous! I cannot think that anything in our behavior compromises our reputations."

"I did not say it did," Daphne said. "You and I, and no doubt all the village, know that the Grant household is respectable, but you and I and the village are not insane with jealousy, Amelia."

"Explain yourself," Amelia said.

"Amelia," Daphne said, drawing close and lowering her voice to barely above a whisper, "you are the elder sister. It is your place to explain the truths of the world to me and not the other way round. Yet I do sometimes think that you and Berdine and Clarisse are as innocent as babes."

"What are you saying?"

"Amelia, dear, the marchioness does not visit at Sir Richard's home in order to pursue her study of his family portraits. She visits and prolongs her stays because she has interests that Berdine would insist cannot be put in words but can only be referred to as sinful."

Amelia was not that innocent. She knew well enough that the *ton* did not live by the moral standards of the good folk of Pickerton Cross or Puddleafton. Yet she did not care to think that the tales that amused housemaids could be applied to the Wyland estate. If they were, it might well be that even the influence of Berdine could not save Sir Richard. She would not sacrifice her sister to the chance of such a fate.

"You think it more than tattle?" she asked Daphne.

Daphne shrugged, tucked her skirt more tightly into her apron strings, and squatted down by a bean row. Her darting fingers loosened weed blades without disturbing the bean roots. "I think Sir Richard is the dearest of men. I also think, if you are really asking what I think, that he finds the marchioness amusing and her daughter company for his son. I do not think he loves her. She wishes that he did and seeks reasons for his disinterest. You have provided her with a target for her anger, Amelia."

"I?"

"Perhaps not you only, but rather, you, our home here, Clarisse, Berdine, and our school which gives him frequent excuse to be away from his estate and from her. I know no other word for her behavior than jealousy."

Amelia did not bother to wonder at young Daphne's wisdom. Daphne had seldom accepted others' opinions. She had ever watched and listened and formed her own mind. The only amazement was that Daphne's thoughts no longer confined themselves to those subjects suitable to children. Until now her originality had touched on table manners, clothing, speech, and daily behavior, creating her own revisions of all rules. But she had been disinterested in the world of relationships between males and females. Or so Amelia had thought. Rather than risk learning what she would not care to know, Amelia did not question her further.

And worse, if the village spread tattle, how would it affect the schoolroom?

Amelia learned the answer to that worry too soon. The next three days brought Mrs. Tupper and three other mothers to her doorstep with awkwardly worded explanations.

Mrs. Tupper said, "With the summer almost on us, I must have the girls at home. We may well have summer visitors, you understand, dear Miss Grant, and I must prepare their clothing."

Another mother said that with the spring turning-out of mattresses and carpets, she had need of her five-year-old child, leaving Amelia to try to imagine the small girl dragging heavy household objects to the back garden for airing. Another said that her daughter had learned quite enough and needed now to remain home to watch a younger child. All seemed embarrassed, yet sure of their mission. Amelia could only nod and politely agree.

Did they doubt her reputation? She refused to believe it.

Berdine said gently, "I fear that many entered their children so that they might be acquainted with Lady Isabelle."

Amelia accepted that explanation as the most satisfactory. She had lived in villages all her life and knew too well the longing of villagers to mingle with the titled. In that respect she knew that their ambitions were not far different from her own. All wished to grasp at any advantage that would someday make more eligible a daughter, for what else could the future hold for a girl? If she did not marry well, she would have a lifetime of suffering and deprivation. Only the daughters of the very rich, such as Aunt Sophie, could afford the luxury of other choices.

At last only Anne Measure and two other girls remained as students.

Once, when Amelia and Daphne were alone, Daphne said, "A pity Sir Richard is still in London. You could send for him and he would soon enough end any foolish rumors."

"Daphne!" Amelia had cried. "Give me your solemn word that you will speak of none of this to Sir Richard. If he decides that the others withdrew because they had enrolled only to be near Lady Isabelle, that is embarrassing enough. My pride requires me to believe we have more to offer in instruction than mere social connections. But to have him told of village chatter! No, Daphne, I forbid it."

"He would laugh," Daphne said. "I know he would, Amelia. He would find it most amusing that the stunning marchioness envied the poor Misses Grant."

"Not a word!" Amelia commanded.

"As you wish. I shall fade quietly away, dying of starvation, but not a word of protest shall pass my lips," Daphne vowed.

The threat was not as idle as Daphne thought. Amelia sat late at the desk, bent over her accounts, her candle flickering and sputtering its precious wax. Tuitions for three children could not be stretched to feed the Grant household. Soon debts would again accumulate.

In her last letter Aunt Sophie had said that she would remain in Bath until the first of June. When she did arrive in Puddleafton and her presence made quite clear the social acceptability of the Grants, as it surely would, villagers would wish again to press such good connections. Amelia felt sure they would. Perhaps a few would return their children during the summer months. By summer's end all would be better. Yes, she felt quite confident. It was not as though anyone had complained at the quality of instruction.

Then she frowned again at the shadowy account book. A few more tuitions in summer would not carry them through until autumn.

She must do something now. With a sigh Amelia put away her account book, locked up the desk, and carried her candle up to her bedchamber.

Lying on her back staring into the dark, Amelia wondered why Sir Richard had gone to London at all. How strange that he should have left without saying farewell. Certainly he need give her no explanation of why or where he traveled. Certainly he was free to relieve his boredom or journey out for any other reason. Yet he might have mentioned his leaving. As she saw him several times each week, it did seem strange that he should leave without a word.

And why now, when Amelia so needed her, did Aunt Sophie's old complaint return, causing her to remain in Bath beyond her usual stay to take the healing waters? The situation was truly vexing. But of course Aunt Sophie thought they were well settled, and besides, Amelia had made it very clear to her that she, Amelia, and not Aunt Sophie, was responsible for the welfare of the Grants.

And so she was. Settling herself into her tatting-edged pillows, Amelia decided what she must do. With but three children, Berdine could handle instruction. Clarisse could relieve her with tatting projects. Daphne needed more time in the garden. It was now beyond an amusement. Daphne could raise much of their food needs. That left their one need of money with which to pay debts for the items they absolutely required.

What they did not need was Amelia. Puddleafton, with its smallness and safeness, was quite suitable as a spot in which to leave her sisters.

It was simple, after all. Tomorrow she would write to Aunt Sophie to explain that her three sisters were nicely managing the school and that she, Amelia, for monetary reasons, required a temporary position as a governess. She knew that such positions did not pay well, yet they did pay something, and the household would have one less mouth to feed.

There was no reason to explain further to Aunt Sophie. Her aunt would assume that Amelia knew what she was about, and if she knew of such a position, she would recommend Amelia.

Yes, that would certainly aid them in this time of distress. Greatly relieved, Amelia let her mind drift toward sleep.

She awoke with a start, remembering Sir Richard. Would he not, when he returned from London, demand to know of the marchioness why she had removed Lady Isabelle from the schoolroom? And what would the marchioness say to him? She could not tell him that she disapproved the instruction, as he had thought it excellent, or so he had said often to Amelia. She could not say anything of the jealousy that Daphne believed prompted her action. What would she say?

And what would Sir Richard believe?

CHAPTER 13

Aunt Sophie's reply came within days of Amelia's query. She did, indeed, know of a family who required a governess, as theirs had left suddenly to attend a bedridden parent. If Amelia was absolutely sure that she wished such a position, though Aunt Sophie could not imagine why she should, then of course she must make her own decision.

With more than a few doubts and misgivings, and hours of serious talks with Berdine and Clarisse as to their responsibilities, Amelia bade her sisters farewell. Sir Archdrake Mandeville of Mandeville Hall sent his carriage to collect her.

Mandeville Hall lay west of Puddleafton toward the sea. It was a day's journey, a distance that kept Amelia within the same corner of England, yet put her too far from Puddleafton for return visits.

"As Aunt Sophie will be at her country house within the fortnight, you must depend on her, though I trust you will not disturb her with household worries. And you must not mention money to her," Amelia warned Berdine. "We cannot accept money from her and still retain our independence."

To Amelia's surprise Berdine agreed completely.

She seemed as eager as Amelia to retain independence. Why Berdine should wish to avoid the fate of succumbing to Aunt Sophie's wishes, Amelia did not know. However, she had suspicions. Berdine knew that Aunt Sophie would never permit her to marry a curate, a marriage that virtually bound a woman to a life of near poverty. Could Berdine possibly be thinking of such a marriage? Did she not know that Amelia, in this case, would be in total agreement with Aunt Sophie?

Amelia added firmly, "Aunt Sophie will be inviting you to her house for various social occasions, Berdine. It is my express wish that you accept all invitations from her."

Berdine said softly, "Of course I shall do so, Amelia. I would not allow Clarisse to attend a social function by herself. You must not worry. I shall be with her and help her as best I can. I truly hope Aunt Sophie will introduce her to a suitable gentleman."

"Yes. You must do that. And I count on you to help her choose appropriate dress," Amelia said, not adding that she also hoped that Berdine would meet a gentleman who would remove the curate from her thoughts.

"Perhaps the viscount will continue to call here," Berdine said, "and Sir Richard, when he returns from London. What am I to do with them?"

Berdine wore her squirrel expression, her round face pinched with worry, her brown eyes puzzled. Amelia patted her shoulder. "Invite them to tea as we have done in the past, dear. But if either suggests taking you for carriage rides or to the shops, I think you must only go in twos. Neither of you must be seen alone with any gentleman."

"Indeed, no!" Berdine said, shocked.

"If a social situation arises that you know not how to handle, *that* is when I wish you to send word to Aunt Sophie and await her advice."

"I shall," Berdine promised. She caught Amelia's hands, rose up on her toes, and kissed Amelia's cheek. "Dear Amelia, I wish you were not leaving. As you must, promise to care well for yourself. I shall write daily and wait anxiously for your return."

"I think that to write daily would cost more dearly than we can pay," Amelia said. "But I shall write when I can and you, also."

She bade her sisters good-bye and hurried out to the carriage, hoping they had not seen the tears that burned beneath her lids. Despite her determination her stomach fluttered miserably. She kept her back straight and her chin high until the carriage crossed the bridge, turned past the spreading tree, and rumbled out of Puddleafton. Then she sank back against the cushions and let her tears slide down her nose untended. She had never before traveled without her sisters, or at least one of them. At the last moment some disturbance at Mandeville Hall had made it quite impossible for the intended housemaid to journey in the carriage to accompany her.

The coachman had explained, "Lady Mandeville has sent a message, Miss Grant."

The short note said only that Amelia was to bring with her an abigail who would then be returned to Puddleafton by stagecoach. As that would have delayed the journey, forcing Amelia to seek out a servant who could be spared, she told the coachman that as they would arrive at Mandeville Hall before nightfall, she would travel alone.

"Yes, miss," he had assured her, "we will certainly do that if we leave at once."

And they had. As the sun was turning the horizon a deep gold and casting its lavender shadows over the rolling meadowland, the carriage turned into the long, rhododendron-lined lane to Mandeville Hall. Amelia had dried her eyes, watched the passing farmlands, and even fallen into short sleeps from which she woke with her neck aching. Now she straightened her bonnet, smoothed out her skirts, and gave her slipper toes a quick dusting with her petticoat ruffle.

She had never before seen a large estate at any distance closer than the passing road. Mandeville Hall rose like a neglected abbey, which, in fact, it was, a gathering of stone towers, peaks, and falling walls. The sunset turned its rough gray surface to orange and purple, so that it looked like an enormous mound of garden stones meant only to form a background for the brilliant flowering shrubs. Beyond the rhododendrons the grounds looked neglected, weed-bound, and vine tangled.

As the coachman helped her down, she asked, "Is the hall very old?"

"Yes, miss. Dates back to the Henrys. 'Twas an abbey, hear say, came down through an earl or maybe a duke, had more'n one name change. Been belonging to the Mandevilles for three generations."

The door, wide enough to drive a carriage through if it weren't for the stone stairs, creaked open. The weight of its carved heraldic symbols seemed to drag its massive iron hinges. A maidservant led Amelia across the enormous stone entry hall to a rear staircase, then up two flights to a small room that contained a bed, a chest, two chairs, and an ancient cupboard. The cupboard appeared to have been fire blackened in the distant past.

"Won't rub off," the maid said. "We've oiled it down, miss, so you needn't worry about your gowns. There's hot water in your pitcher if you'd like a wash. First door down the hall is the schoolroom. Beyond that is Master John's door and next on is his nanny."

"There's but one child?" Amelia asked.

"Three, miss. Other side of the nanny is the girls' room. Miss Susan and Miss Charlotte. Will you be taking your tea in the schoolroom or in the nursery?"

"What did the previous governess do?"

"Took it alone in the schoolroom, miss."

"Oh, I shouldn't like that!" Amelia exclaimed.

The girl gave her a look of pity. "Nanny won't much fancy having you in the nursery."

"Oh. I see. Well, then, perhaps I could have my tea here."

"Here?" The maid looked about. "You'll need a table, miss."

"Would that be difficult?"

The maid met Amelia's eyes and suddenly smiled. She was a girl, no older than Daphne. "No, miss," she said. "I'll find one for you. If you like, I could lay a bit of fire in your hearth."

"In May?" Amelia exclaimed. "That's very kind, but I couldn't let you do that."

"Don't usually, miss," the girl said. "But seeing it's your first night."

"Will no one mind?"

"Who's to tell?" the maid said, and disappeared. By the time Amelia had removed and smoothed her

158

wraps and emptied the contents of her trunk into the cupboard and chest, the girl had found a small table, arranged it beneath the window, laid a wood fire, and brought Amelia a tray of supper.

"You're very kind," Amelia said. "What name are you called?"

"Sloan," she said.

"I have a sister who is fourteen. You look her age."

Sloan grinned. "Do you, miss? I be a year more."

Amelia wished she could invite Sloan to sit down with her and keep her company, but she knew she could not. The Mandevilles would be most unhappy if she disrupted the discipline of the household staff. She said, "Thank you, Sloan, for your thoughtfulness."

"You're welcome, I'm sure," Sloan said. She bobbed her head and hurried out.

Amelia sat alone gazing out the window. She could see across the land in back of the Hall a meadow that rolled down into a languid river, where it turned to forestland. The dark trees blended into the dark sky and disappeared. The stars shone faintly, then brighter. When she could see nothing at all except the stars, Amelia wandered over to the hearth and held out her hands to the embers. Sloan had laid a small fire and spread it out so that it would not flame too high or send a pouring of smoke up the chimney, and had cautioned Amelia not to stir it. The fire must be against the household rules this late in the year, Amelia concluded.

For the first time she realized that she was totally alone in her role as governess. She was neither a guest nor a servant. She was of the gentry, which

159

made it impossible for her to befriend the servants, yet she was unlikely to be included with the family or guests for social gatherings. What was it that governesses did when they were not in the schoolroom with the children, she wondered.

She found out in the morning and it did not please her. If she had not planned to remain only the summer, she would have been tempted to walk to the next village and immediately find a stagecoach to return her to Puddleafton.

Shortly after she had breakfasted, the nanny rapped on her door and introduced herself.

"The children will be in the schoolroom at nine o'clock," she said, carefully separating her syllables. "They will remain with you until noon, when they will return to the nursery for their meal. You shall instruct them again from two until four."

"And what shall I do at four?" Amelia asked.

Nanny, who was small and had the face of last year's dried apples, sniffed. "It is not for me to instruct you," she said, lifting her nose as though to test the purity of the air. She then turned and marched back to the nursery.

The children proved to be pleasant enough, if rather shy, with faded light brown hair and faded complexions, small for their ages and very weak in their schooling. They sat quietly, listened to what she said, then promptly forgot everything.

Amelia tried to remember some of the ditties Daphne sang to the small girls, though these children were older. Susan was ten, John nine, and Charlotte six.

"We don't know how to sing," Susan said seriously.

"Then I shall teach you."

"Yes, Miss Grant," they said in unison. Unfortunately, that was all they could do in unison. They could remember neither words nor tunes, sang in different ranges of flat tone, and recalled different lines.

Still, they could have been rude or unpleasant. As it was, they were only dull.

At four o'clock, after they had returned to the nursery, Sloan came to fetch Amelia. She led her downstairs and into a small side-parlor where a dark, somber woman with scowl lines in her forehead sat waiting.

"Miss Grant," she said, "I am Mrs. Foresster, the housekeeper. If you have any queries, you will direct them to me. I presume your room is satisfactory?"

"Yes, thank you, Mrs. Foresster."

The woman nodded. "Very well. Lady Mandeville wishes to meet you now. You will follow me."

After a night and day of seeing no one but Sloan, nanny, and the children, Amelia had begun to wonder if there was a Lady Mandeville. Or a Sir Archdrake. The thought had crossed her mind that they might be elsewhere, perhaps in London or Bath.

There was indeed a Lady Mandeville. She was not quite what Amelia had expected, having formed a picture of someone who would fit into Aunt Sophie's drawing room.

Lady Mandeville could best be described as handsome but not pretty, being tall and solidly built, with large hands and feet. Her facial features were strong, casting interesting shadows, with an arched nose and full mouth. Her eyes and hair were blue-black. How she had managed to produce such faded children puzzled Amelia.

"Ah, Miss Grant," Lady Mandeville shouted, though Amelia was quite close to her. "How very pleasant to meet you. You are in some way related to Miss Stafford, I understand."

"She is my great-aunt," Amelia explained.

"Yes, yes, I see, she is a dear friend of my mother's sister, I believe, or somesuch. Never can keep all of Mama's bosom friends sorted. How good of you to come. What we would have done, I cannot tell! That last governess, oh, I can't remember her name, Mrs. Foresster can tell you, anyway, she left us high and dry! High and dry! No good expecting Nanny to teach the children a thing, she can barely read, you see, but the silly old thing has been in the family forever. Not my family! Sir Archdrake's family. Can't think why they kept her. Still, she keeps the children out from underfoot and I always say that a nanny who can do that is worth her weight, yes?"

The whole speech was delivered at a pitch that should have carried well past the doors that Mrs. Foresster had carefully closed after she introduced Amelia and then withdrew. Amelia hoped that nanny was not lurking in the hall.

"I am sure she is very capable," Amelia said uncertainly, wondering what was expected of her now.

Lady Mandeville cleared up that problem. She said, "Now, then, dear, you'll come take tea with me each day. Don't like to sit about alone."

She did not, in fact, *sit about* much and *alone* almost not at all. In the days that followed, Amelia discovered that Lady Mandeville paced constantly while shouting comments. The room was occasionally empty. Then her ladyship directed her words to Amelia. More often it filled with callers. Then Amelia apparently became invisible, because after a nod in her direction, visitors pretended she was not there. That may have been because Lady Mandeville never introduced her. Whatever the reason, Amelia was at first deeply disturbed by her role. To be ignored was discomfiting. But once she had learned to expect it, she found the role educational. She removed herself a small distance from the circle of visitors, choosing a chair near the wall, and relaxed back into its stiff height to observe the crowd as one might observe a performance at a theater.

The drawing room of Mandeville Hall had been dusted regularly during the past three hundred years, but that seemed to be all that had been done to it. Beneath the gloomy, gray-arched stone ceiling the room stretched from the most massive fireplace Amelia had ever seen to tall narrow windows that framed views of the overgrown garden. The furniture was the heavy black stuff of Elizabethan times, with chair backs shaped like Gothic arches and cupboards boasting bulbous legs and carved doors. From the carvings peered boars' heads and angry faces.

Had Lady Mandeville and her guests been soft-spoken people, the whole effect would have been one of a medieval monastery. Instead, the place more nearly resembled what Amelia had imagined Bedlam to be like.

Lady Mandeville and her guests outshouted each other, laughed wildly at jests that concerned animals and neighbors, and waved their arms as they spoke. Their main interest seemed to be horses. Their second interest was hunting.

"Got seven of the bloody things," Lady Mandeville shouted to the half dozen guests that paced the room with her. "Hung their tails on the stable door to dry. Sent the groom into fits! Said they scared the horses!"

The guests howled. Amelia slid deeper into the shadows of her enormous Gothic chair. She seemed to be the only person in the room who drank tea. Although two ladies held teacups, Amelia had seen them fill the cups with sherry from the decanter. The men and Lady Mandeville drank their spirits from crystal wineglasses.

"Course they scared the horses!" bellowed Lord Roderick, a heavy, red-faced man who called several times a week. "What didja expect? I vow, Eleanora, you're the only female in England who'd tack foxtails to a stable and expect the horses to like it!"

He and Lady Mandeville and all the other guests doubled up with laughter, as though he had said the most clever thing. Only Sir Archdrake contained his amusement to a half smile. Now that Amelia had met him, she knew whom the children resembled. He was, if possible, more faded than the children, a shadow who spent his time glass in hand, his dull, red-rimmed eyes half closed, nodding in agreement to his wife's steady stream of talk.

Despite her complete confusion at the behavior in the drawing room, Amelia rather liked Sir Archdrake and Lady Mandeville. They seemed kind. Certainly they in no way criticized her. For that matter they did not actually talk to her. Lady Mandeville talked *at* her, but not about Amelia or any matter that concerned Amelia. So it was somewhat surprising when Lady Mandeville did send for her one day and said, "M'dear, as you no doubt heard, there will be a rout-party here come Saturday. Occurs to me you may not have proper dress. Am sending my dressmaker up to check. Take what she offers."

Amelia said, "That's most kind, Lady Mandeville, but there is no need to include me in the party."

"Not include you!" her ladyship cried. "Course I do. It's expected. Never enough young females, all the men say so. Course you must attend. Run along now. See the dressmaker. Not another word."

As Lady Mandeville had swept past Amelia and sailed across the hallway by the time she had finished that speech, Amelia could not protest. She remembered Aunt Sophie's modiste, who had attempted to dress Clarisse and herself in gowns that Amelia would have been embarrassed to wear to bed, and she feared a similar occurrence with this dressmaker. Lady Mandeville's necklines plunged beyond proper description, revealing most of her full, solid bosom.

Amelia could not even sort out her feelings in her letters to her sisters. She did not wish to worry them, so she wrote only that the children were pleasant and her room comfortable. That night she mentioned that she had been invited to join the party, without saying a word about the dressmaker. As she read over her letter before sealing it, she wondered how much Berdine left out of letters to herself. Berdine reported of progress in lessons, said the garden was doing well, that Clarisse seemed more cheerful.

Of Mr. Edmond Chicore and Mr. John Measure, Berdine wrote not a word. Amelia fervently hoped that those two gentlemen had disappeared from her sisters' lives and thoughts. Berdine did say that Aunt Sophie would return to her country house within a few days, having again delayed her departure from Bath. And she mentioned that the viscount had called twice.

If he continued to call, Amelia felt safe to presume that he had definite thoughts on his mind other than sharing their tea.

And in one brief, very unsatisfactory sentence, Berdine said, "Sir Richard is still in London."

Amelia had touched his written name on the page, drawn away her finger in dismay, folded the letter, and put it out of sight. It was as well that he was gone. Better yet if he remained the summer in London. The more she thought of the village tattle, the less she wished him connected with her family. With him gone, perhaps Berdine would meet some proper gentleman, one who did not dally with the wives of friends, one who would outcharm Mr. Measure. Surely Aunt Sophie could find such a person. Amelia regretted that she could not be there to help arrange such meetings.

With a sigh she gazed from her window at the darkening forest and wished away the summer. From this distance all she could do for her sisters was worry.

CHAPTER 14

Lady Mandeville's cheerful neglect extended to all facets of her behavior, Amelia discovered. Lady Mandeville had insisted that Amelia appear at tea each day, and then had ignored her. She fussed about the qualification of Nanny, yet did no more for her children than pat them on the head each evening when they were brought to her for their good-nights. She overwhelmed her guests and family with her opinions, yet left the running of her house completely to the housekeeper.

And so, to Amelia's relief, Lady Mandeville made her one statement about Amelia and the dressmaker, then completely forgot the subject. The dressmaker never asked for Amelia and Amelia did not go looking for the dressmaker. She took out the dark-blue gown that she had worn to Aunt Sophie's party in Bath. It was the only party dress she had brought with her. Aunt Sophie had also had cut for her a very ruffly gown of peach muslin, but Amelia considered it far too young and had given it to Berdine to cut down for herself.

On the evening of the party Amelia dressed in her high-throated, long-sleeved, dark-blue gown, the very one she had worn when she first danced with Sir

Richard. He had commented that it was a clever choice, that in a room full of pale, clinging gowns it definitely caught the eye.

Amelia stamped her foot. This constant thinking of Sir Richard was an irritating habit, one she must break. She tied her pale-green silk sash below her bosom and caught back her dark curls in a matching ribbon. Her reflection glowed back at her from the mirror above her washstand, the candlelight sparkling in her bright blue eyes. Her face was a pale circle, its expression so serious that the dimple at the corner of her lower lip did not show. Her small chin was firm with determination. She would attend the party, fade into the background as much as possible, and learn what she could of the correct behavior at country parties. She would look on this evening as an educational experience to be shared with her sisters to their benefit and enlightenment.

She sincerely hoped that her dark dress would help her disappear into the shadows of Mandeville Hall. She had no wish to dance with any of the noisy gentlemen who called here. The thought that one might ask her sent the blood flowing to her cheeks, and their softly rounded shape, glowing pink, made Amelia look much younger and prettier than she realized.

When she heard music drifting through the old abbey, music so lively that it must have startled the ancient ghosts of the monks, if they still lurked about, Amelia went downstairs. She used the back servants' stairs, though Lady Mandeville had told her that she need not do that. Amelia preferred the dark, narrow stairs. She could move down them unobserved 'and look into the front hallway to see who was there before they saw her.

The entry blazed with color. Multistemmed candelabras perched on tables, stands, and niches, their peaks of tiny flames blending into arches of light, casting glitter and shadow. The hearth, a hole in the stone wall that was as wide as a carriage and taller than a man, held a small forest of logs, their fire crackling loudly. Swarms of people, women in bright muslins of butterfly colors and flowing silks in jewel tones of green and ruby, men in velvet and burnished leather, milled about. Some wore wigs. Many wore so much ruffled lace that they looked like walking pillow slips. All wore jewels. Emeralds, diamonds, and sapphires sparkled at throats and on gesturing hands. In some cases the men outdid the women.

Amelia supposed she was the only person present who wore not a single jewel. Her only jewel was a small emerald ring of her mother's, and she had left it with Berdine, presuming that a governess should not wear jewels. She had not thought she might be required to attend such a lavish party.

The drawing room had been turned into a ballroom, its dark furnishings pushed back against its stone walls. Musicians filled one small corner. The rest of its enormous, and usually empty, space overflowed with richly dressed guests. Their perfumes outweighed each other until scents, smoke, food, and liquor fumes almost choked Amelia.

The doors to the dining hall stood open. The tables could barely be seen beneath the array of platters, some so heavy that Amelia thought it must take two footmen to carry them in from the kitchens. Whole boars, roasts, and stuffed fowl, mountains of breads,

169

cakes, and richly spiced vegetable concoctions, as well as overflowing baskets of fruits, gleamed in the candleglow. People did not move sedately into the ballroom to dance, be introduced, change partners, as they had at the party at Sir Richard's grandmother's home. No one announced a supper hour. Gentlemen did not escort ladies to the tables or bring them neat platters of food.

Instead, the guests milled in the entry shouting greetings, dashed into the ballroom, grabbed each other, and pranced through disorganized country dances. They fell into each other's arms with most unseemly abandon, tottering out to the dining hall to overload their platters and refill their goblets. Amelia watched, wide eyed, and shrank back into the shadows.

Lady Mandeville sailed by, a vast expanse of bosom displayed above her clinging rose silk gown with its fluttering back panels and its wide wrist ruffles of gold lace. Diamonds sparkled at her throat, ears, wrists, and fingers. Her black hair rose, mound upon twisted mound, held in place with ribbons, feathers, and jeweled clips. On each side of her a ruffled gentleman in a dark velvet coat, shining silk vest, tight pantaloons, and striped silk stockings, scurried to keep apace. She shouted to them both at once and they nodded wildly.

"Best, best, best, doncha think, m'dear? Never liked that waltz thing! Can't abide silly fingerfoods, half a bite apiece. Now that's a tune! Say, who's that one? Oh, yes, always do forget her name. Can't think why he married her! Can't even 'sit a horse,' hear tell!"

Appalled and fascinated, Amelia watched Lady

Mandeville rush around the table, leaning over to snatch a bit of pork in her fingertips and pop it into her mouth. Then she saw that many of the guests did the same, not bothering with plates. A moment later her ladyship marched off to the ballroom and joined a set, grabbing one of the gentlemen who shadowed her and leaving the other to stand aside, watching.

At Amelia's side someone cleared his throat. Amelia shivered, startled.

"Sorry, m'dear, didn't mean to give you the fright," Sir Archdrake said sadly. His faded features all but disappeared above the lavish neck ruff. His coat was a brilliant green, his waistcoat heavily embroidered.

"Good evening, Sir Archdrake," Amelia stammered. "It—it's a lovely party."

"Hardly started," he said. "Care to join a set?"

"Oh, I really—I hardly know how to dance."

"Not dance?" He peered into her face, puzzled, then shrugged. "Doesn't matter, miss. None of the rest can, either."

"I—I feel a bit out of place. Everyone is so elegant."

"Nonsense, if that's all that worries you. You look lovely," he said, and tucked her hand through his arm.

Amelia trailed along with him, thinking she would dance this once, then return to her room. She would not for anything hurt his feelings, as he seemed a kind gentleman.

However, she misjudged the rest of the party. No sooner had Sir Archdrake bowed his thanks at the dance's end then another guest claimed her hand and whirled her into the next dance.

"What's your name?" he shouted above the music and chatter.

"Miss Grant," she said, wondering what had become of the old rules of behavior when a gentleman asked a lady's name through the hostess or chaperone before requesting her to stand up with him.

"Sweet name," he said, and she knew he had not heard her reply.

Although she had at first suspected that he was rude and an exception, she soon discovered that he was typical of the guests. Perhaps it was because most lived nearby and knew each other well, but no one supplied any introductions and the gentlemen exchanged partners without asking permission of the ladies. The other ladies seemed quite satisfied with this arrangement.

All the guests by now smelled strongly of spirits. Amelia decided that that also might explain their unusual manners. But as she had no real experience with people who imbibed, she could not be sure. Despite her father's weakness for gaming, he was not a drinking man.

Each time Amelia tried to duck out of the ballroom, another gentleman blocked her way and insisted that she be his partner. By now the guests were falling against each other, laughing wildly. They caught Amelia's hands so tightly that her fingers ached and she was glad she did not wear a ring. They stamped on her toes. They caught her about the waist and swung her so quickly into the next step that she stumbled several times.

"They will think I have been drinking, too," she muttered, having found that she could freely voice her thoughts as no one could hear her above the music and shouted laughter.

When the music finally broke, Lady Mandeville screamed above the chatter, "Can't do it, Wickle! Can't be done. Hear that, didja, says he can outride me! Never heard such!"

The howls of gaiety echoed in the vaulted ceilings. Someone shouted a challenge.

"You're on!" Lady Mandeville cried, and the crowd surged through the garden windows, carrying Amelia with them. She gulped with relief at the fresh night air.

"She'll do it, too," a heavy, liquor-breathed man panted into Amelia's ear. She could feel the heated flush of his face almost touching hers. She tried to dodge but found herself caught in the crowd.

"There she goes!"

People ran in all directions, shouting, applauding, waving jeweled hands and fans and lace shawls above their heads. They separated enough to allow Amelia to see.

Five horses galloped up the drive and past the crowd, then sped over the darkened hill toward some unseen goal. Lady Mandeville, her rose silk panels floating behind her like a cape, held the lead. Two gentlemen and another lady sat the three other mounts and one ran without a rider. Amelia wondered if someone had been thrown.

"Fifty guineas on her ladyship," a voice shouted, and was drowned out by matched bets.

Amelia edged through the weaving, stumbling guests, making her way back to the windows and into the ballroom. The musicians were gone, but as she reached the entry hall she saw them in the dining hall, filling platters. She had almost reached the stairs when a hand caught her about the waist and swung her into a tight grip. She found herself crushed against an enormous silk-striped stomach.

"Let me go," she gasped, pushing frantically.

A flushed, foul-smelling face bent to hers. Amelia ducked her face into the velvet coat. She did not know who the man was. All the guests were fat, flushed, overdressed, and reeked of a variety of odors. She tried to wedge her elbows into his ribs, but could not get her arms loose.

"Pretty gel," he mumbled, his hands pulling at her sleeves. Amelia feared the frail muslin would give way quickly.

Frantic, she pulled back one slippered foot and aimed it with all her strength at him. Her toe collided with his shin.

"My gawd! Wicked wench!" he cried, his one arm loosening.

Amelia felt her sash rip away from her bodice. In desperation she twisted quickly and brought her teeth together on his hand.

While he shrieked in pain, she broke loose and raced up the back staircase.

Her heart pounded wildly. Her breath burned in her throat. She ran up three flights without stopping before she dared pause for breath. Then she heard him slowly lumbering around on the lower stairs.

A voice said, "Never you mind, miss, he won't come farther."

Amelia thought she would die. She grabbed the bannister, steadied herself, then recognized the voice.

Above her on the landing stood Sloan, a water pitcher in her hand.

"You go on to your room," she said. "If he comes any farther, I'll give him a wash. And if that don't stop him, he'll get the pitcher."

"Oh, Sloan! Are you sure you'll be all right?"

Sloan chuckled. "Been through these parties before, miss. Don't fret. I know my way."

"Thank you ever so much," Amelia gasped, and stumbled into her room. After closing the door, she slid her washstand in front of it. If anyone tried to open it, the crashing of the bowl and pitcher would give them pause, she hoped.

Where was the housekeeper while all this went on? Amelia sank into her chair by the window. Were the parties always so terrible? She leaned out the opening to cool her face in the soft air. The night smelled of flowering shrubs, damp earth, and the river at the bottom of the garden.

Then she heard a shriek followed by more laughter. In the starlight she saw the dark shapes of four horses and riders. The riderless mount must have wandered off elsewhere.

Lady Mandeville still held the lead. Her long black hair streamed back, freed from its ribbons and clips. She was laughing wildly.

Amelia sighed. Apparently this household did not consider their parties unusual. No doubt the housekeeper and servants kept themselves in the kitchens out of sight. Very wise of them. Amelia decided she would do the same.

She fingered her torn dress, wondering if it could be repaired. The tear had gone past the seam, following the material's thread across her bosom and over her shoulder. She feared there was little she could do for it except pack it away. Berdine might know how to mend it, disguising the torn bodice beneath a frill of tatting. But how would she explain the damage?

And even if the dress could be repaired, Amelia doubted that she would ever again feel comfortable in it. It would remind her of the dreadful crush of rude men and the hateful, vile, beastly man who had tried to trap her in the lower hall.

Men, Amelia decided, were useful enough if one kept them confined to the well-chaperoned drawing room and only saw them during daylight hours. Aunt Sophie was quite right to choose an independent life.

Fingering her crushed sash, Amelia wondered if she would be able to afford to avoid matrimony. She desperately wished to do so as she had no desire to take on a man with his gaming, drinking, and other bad habits, having had quite enough worry with her father. She must make her school successful. For the first time since leaving Puddleafton she ached with homesickness.

If only she could return now. But she needed the money promised her if she remained the summer. Her every desire urged her to pack her trunk and send for the carriage. But her common sense reminded her of the debts that must be paid.

Perhaps tomorrow's post would bring a letter from Berdine. She hoped so. Any word was better than this lonely existence.

Or so she thought before she received her next letter.

In the morning she dressed carefully in her dark gray, and smoothed her curls as much as she could, though they did tend to froth away from her face and fall about her cheeks of their own will. She tied them with a plain white ribbon. After breakfasting from a tray brought by a weary Sloan, Amelia led the children through a very structured lesson, reading aloud and then asking them to recite. In the afternoon she gave them sums to work on their slates. They bent their heads obediently and Amelia felt guilty. Usually she spent time telling them stories, singing, or playing a game of ring-the-rose, but this morning she did not feel up to it.

When she had dismissed them, she returned to her room to freshen up, then hesitated to go to the drawing room. Could she face Lady Mandeville? What if that obnoxious man who had grabbed her now came to call?

Gathering her courage, Amelia went quietly down the back stairs. When she reached the entry hall, she was confronted with the confusion of servants carrying furnishings back to their original places. A maidservant knelt at the mammoth hearth scooping ashes into a bucket. Three menservants swished mops across the stone floor. Two others carried out a rolled carpet.

The housekeeper stood in the center, saying clearly, "Give it a good beating and then sweep it down with wet brooms."

Sloan rushed past with a mop and pail, saw Amelia, and whispered, "Best stay abovestairs, miss. Housekeeper's in her usual fret after a do. Her ladyship won't be down."

But before Amelia could return to the stairs, the housekeeper spotted her. "Miss Grant," she said sharply. "There's a letter for you. I have not had a maid to spare to carry it up to you." She pulled a wrinkled envelope from her pocket and handed it to Amelia.

"Thank you," Amelia said. "Is there anything that I can do to assist?"

"I hardly think so," Mrs. Foresster said, looking at her sharply and then obviously dismissing her as useless. She marched off to instruct a servant.

Amelia had intended to carry her letter back to her room before opening it, but as she glanced down, she saw her name written in Berdine's hand and also saw that the hand that wrote had been visibly shaking. Worried that Berdine might be suffering from a summer fever, she unfolded the page.

"Amelia, dearest," Berdine wrote, "I am quite out of my depth, I fear, but you must not overly concern yourself on my account, as there seems little you can do to alter the situation. A Mr. Edmond Chicore arrived quite unannounced this morning while I was busy with the girls. Clarisse went out to speak to him. Although I did hear her once mention his name, I knew not that there was reason to chaperone them at all times, thus I unwisely left her alone with him in the front hall and quite forgot them.

"You can well imagine my dismay when, after dismissing the class, I went to find Clarisse and found instead a note from her.

"Amelia, I do not know how to say this. You will not believe it. But Clarisse states in her message that Mr. Chicore has obtained a special license. I do not know what that is, but it would seem to be some sort of permission to marry. And so she has gone off with him, taking her small portmanteau and but a few garments. She did not even bid us farewell!

"I am quite devastated. Knowing not what to do, I have sent off a message to Aunt Sophie as you said I should. She returned to her estate a few days ago. I do regret worrying you with this news. No doubt there is little you can do either, yet I do feel you would have known who and what Mr. Chicore is and would have better handled the situation to avoid such an overwhelming and shocking outcome of his call."

Amelia paled. Her fingers shook so that the paper rattled. She had imagined, in her most unpleasant considerations, that Mr. Chicore might well appear at Puddleafton at some future time. She had hoped that by that time Clarisse would have met more desirable gentlemen at Aunt Sophie's house, or that she would have compared Mr. Chicore to the attentive viscount and realized the shopkeeper's shortcomings.

What she had never imagined, even when she had known she might be called upon to forcefully explain to Mr. Chicore the unacceptability of his interest in Clarisse, was that Mr. Chicore would arrive with a special license and a determination to spirit away Clarisse without even seeking her family's consent.

What sort of beast was he?

A hand touched Amelia's arm. "My dear, have you had a shock?" Sir Archdrake asked.

Amelia's lip quivered. She did so despise it when she could not remain composed. Fighting back the rising tears, she said, "I fear there is drastic trouble at my home." And then, to her own horror, she sniffed loudly. A tear escaped and ran down her cheek.

"I do regret hearing this," he said. "If there is illness, you must, of course, return at once."

"Oh, could I?" she cried, her eyes shining, then caught back her eagerness and asked more quietly, "Would Lady Mandeville be terribly inconvenienced? I have given my word to remain the summer."

"If you ask her, she will be most annoyed," he said. "Go pack your belongings. I shall send up a man to carry them down for you and call round the carriage."

As Amelia hurried to pile her belongings into her trunk, she fought back her fears. Her position in this household had been uncomfortable and she had longed to leave, but she would not have done so if Sir Archdrake had not insisted. An obligation was an obligation and she had never shirked her duty.

Yet when she returned to the lower hallway, she found that not everyone agreed with her.

"So you are leaving, are you?" Mrs. Foresster demanded. "Surprises me not at all. I thought at first meeting that you lacked character."

"I beg your pardon!" Amelia said.

"I will not wake her ladyship to bother her with such a disgusting matter, but I will tell you, young woman, that as you have not honored your agreement, you shall certainly receive no compensation."

Amelia thought it best to ignore the housekeeper. Walking past her and out the front doors, she stared in surprise at the empty drive.

"We've no carriage to spare to drive unreliable servants about the countryside," Mrs. Foresster snapped at her back.

Amelia wheeled about. "Sir Archdrake said the carriage should take me."

"And so it will, at summer's end," the housekeeper said. "If you leave early, it's your own affair."

"Where is Sir Archdrake?" Amelia demanded.

"Gone out for the day, not that it concerns you," the housekeeper said, and with a spiteful smile, she closed the double doors.

Amelia stood, bewildered. It occurred to her that the housekeeper would not have dared speak to her thus had Sir Archdrake been within hearing. There was little she could do. She could await his return, of course, but what if he, like Lady Mandeville, tended to give orders in one breath and forget them in the next? By tonight he might decide she should stay.

Staring down the long drive, Amelia knew she must make a quick decision. She had put on her traveling dress and bonnet, sturdy shoes, and a light cape. In her reticule she had a small sum, enough, she thought, to purchase a return to Puddleafton on a stagecoach.

Or she could remain at Mandeville Hall. If she were needed at Puddleafton, Aunt Sophie would send for her.

Amelia shuddered. She thought of the terrible man and the previous night's party. Was she using Berdine's letter as an excuse to run away?

No. She had intended to stay, and to carefully avoid any further parties, until she received Berdine's letter. So it was not that. The truth was, Clarisse, Berdine, and Daphne were not Aunt Sophie's responsibility. They were hers. She had thought they could manage without her, but they could not. She must return. Later she would worry about the debts.

Perhaps she could sell some of the porcelain. All that mattered now was that she return and once more supervise a household that seemed to be falling apart in her absence.

Lifting her small chin in a determined gesture, she set off down the drive. The gleaming hedges moved softly in the summer breeze.

She did not know the exact distance to the village, but she was sure she could reach it. Indeed, so far as she could see, she had no other choice.

Dust rose from the carriage road beyond the entry gates. Here the sun shone less kindly. Amelia walked on. The sun burned through her cape. She pulled her bonnet forward to better shield her face. The road glimmered into a brilliant blur. She blinked back tears. Her legs began to ache. She feared the flesh on her feet had rubbed raw beneath her slipper toes. Digging into her reticule, she drew out an inadequate handkerchief that consisted mostly of tatting, and blew her nose. As she stood still, tucking the cloth back into her tiny bag, she heard a carriage approach from behind her. She stepped to the side and waited for it to pass, but to her surprise it stopped beside her.

The Mandeville coachman jumped down. Amelia glanced back and knew that she was at least a mile past the Hall's gate.

"I am sorry, miss. I was told to meet you at the door, but then Mrs. Foresster said you wouldn't be going. Only just now Sloan came to tell me you'd started off on your own."

He looked like a guardian angel to Amelia, but she said, "I fear I am not to ride in the carriage. Mrs. Foresster forbade it, though I do not understand why."

The coachman smiled. "Never you mind that, miss. She's jealous, that's all."

"Jealous?" Amelia asked, bewildered.

"Course, miss." He held open the door, then reached over to take her elbow and hand her up into the carriage. As the door latched, he smiled up at her and said, "Started as a scullery, that one did, so she'd give a deal to best a real lady like yourself, ma'm. Now, we're a bit late starting, so I'll just travel through the night and you lean back there and get some sleep."

In her hurry to leave, Amelia had forgotten that it was already midafternoon. She could not possibly travel alone with no maid and one coachman after dark.

"Oh, dear," she cried, "I hadn't realized! It's so late! We must go back and start in the morning."

"Wouldn't advise that, miss. Today I can say I got me orders mixed, but tomorrow—ah, it might be harder to get away. You're not afraid to go alone with me, are you, miss? If it makes you any easier, I'm Sloan's brother."

For the first time Amelia was able to smile back at him. "I see," she said. "Yes, that makes it easier."

"Sloan packed a bit of supper for you. It's on the floor there, and your trunk's on top, so off we go," he said, and she heard him swing up into his seat.

Exhausted by the party and the letter, Amelia sank back into the velvet-lined coach and closed her eyes. Its swaying put her into a light sleep. Her mind drifted, sometimes waking to see the trees flash by, sometimes dreaming uneasily of a party, angry shouting, Lady Mandeville on a horse, and of a letter.

She roused as the sun set. Across wide meadows it turned the sky a deep gold. Opening the packet on the floor of the coach, she found a teapot carefully wrapped in cloths to keep it hot, a cup, and a covered dish filled with cold partridge from last night's party and a slab of fruit pie. Leaning forward, she rapped on the ceiling. The coachman opened the window behind his seat and peered in at her.

"Yes, miss?"

"May I give you some of this supper?" she asked.

"Thank you, miss, I've mine here with me," he said, and closed the window.

When he next spoke to her, it was to reach into the coach to touch her hand. Amelia awoke with a start. Sloan's brother stood by the open door, smiling.

"We're here, miss," he said. "Let me help you down and then I'll fetch your trunk."

Amelia stumbled sleepily from the coach and hurried up the walk. The village was silent. She could see the small cottages that circled the common, black shapes against the dark sky. No candle glimmered anywhere.

Sloan's brother placed her trunk within the hallway, then stepped back out.

"It's so late!" Amelia said. "What will you do now?"

"There's an inn an hour back. I'll stop there. The horses need it. The master gave me the cost." He reached out his hand to her and she felt coins drop into her palm. "He gave me this for you, miss."

"You've been so kind," she said.

"I'd better be," he said, "or Sloan'd have me scalp. Night, miss."

CHAPTER 15

Sir Richard leaned forward in his carriage to better view Amelia's face. She lowered her eyes. This whole journey was quite beyond anything she would have planned or approved a few weeks earlier, but her month at Mandeville Hall and then Clarisse's elopement had disarranged all her lifelong standards.

She had returned home to find Berdine in a perpetual state of tears and Daphne in a perpetual state of gardening. Neither one could enlighten her. Neither one knew Clarisse's whereabouts. So it was with some relief that she opened her door to an unexpected knocking and found Sir Richard smiling down at her as though all the world were in its proper order.

"When Berdine wrote to your great-aunt, she in turn sent word directly to my grandmother, who sent word directly to me. And here I am."

"I cannot think why this should involve you," Amelia said, not meaning to sound ungrateful. At this point, with Berdine still sniffling above stairs, she was grateful for a smiling face.

"You cannot think that either of our elderly relatives could rush here," he said. "No, they have sent me. Rest assured, dear Miss Grant, those two ladies have been using me as their errand lad since the day I was out of skirts."

"But what is to be done?" Amelia asked, trying to keep her voice steady. For a brief moment she had an uncontrollable, unreasonable, and illogical urge to fling herself weeping into his protective arms. As she had never done such an act in her life, she blushed at the thought and stiffened her spine.

"I think it is not quite so terrible as you suppose," he said gently. "Your sister resides in a small village no more than two hours' ride from here. Her new husband owns a shop and lodgings. I will not describe it to you, as I have only hearsay, but I think we will all feel more comfortable about Miss Clarisse when we have viewed the situation for ourselves."

"I—I don't quite take your meaning."

"Miss Grant, my carriage waits. I am suggesting that we spend a day journeying to visit the new Mrs. Edmond Chicore."

Amelia thought she must have presented logical arguments against such a journey. But now, riding in Sir Richard's carriage, she could not remember them. She was dismayed by the lack of chaperone, yet Berdine did not feel well and Daphne said that, although she would love to go, there was some vital thing she needed to do in her garden. Dora insisted that carriage rides made her ill and also that the laundress was arriving. Sir Richard smoothed away all objections, making the unchaperoned trip appear to be the express wish of Aunt Sophie and his grandmother. Amelia, who was worn past arguing, gave in to her real desire to see Clarisse and determine the state of her well-being.

The carriage rolled into a pleasant, tree-lined village, its houses set in deep gardens behind lush hedges, its shops large, with wide, many-paned casements of windows facing the road.

Sir Richard's footman opened the carriage door.

"Why are we stopping at a draper's?" Amelia asked.

"I thought we might first meet Mr. Edmond Chicore," Sir Richard said.

For an awful moment Amelia's heart caught in her throat. Could she face this evil person who had so misled her innocent sister? Yet if she did not meet him, she could in no way aid poor Clarisse. She looked to Sir Richard for reassurance. He smiled, his expression encouraging her.

Within the shop she was amazed to discover its size. It filled quite twice the space of any establishment in Puddleafton or even Pickerton Cross, displaying quality wares. The yard goods and ribbons were most exceptional and a box of gloves on a counter was certainly from France. An elderly woman with silver-gray hair and a kindly face came through the curtains on the rear wall.

"Good morning, sir, madam. May I be of service to you?"

"We require a Mr. Edmond Chicore," Sir Richard said, "if you would be so kind, ma'm."

The woman beamed her willingness, disappeared behind the curtain, and spoke softly to someone there. Who was she, Amelia wondered? Mr. Chicore's sister? Was he, like her, kind faced, gray, plump, and twice Clarisse's age? No, Clarisse had said he was young, or so Amelia recalled, but she could not be sure.

The curtains parted and a young man appeared.

He was not as tall as Sir Richard, but he was comely, with a well-shaped head, golden hair that waved back from his face in a surprisingly neat style, and simple, beautifully tailored clothing. His square face, with its straight brows, pleasant blue eyes, heavy nose, and wide mouth, was quite handsome—perhaps not as handsome as the dashing perfection of the viscount, but handsome in a friendly, trustworthy way that undid Amelia's resolution to dislike him.

"I am Mr. Edmond Chicore," he said. "How may I serve you?"

Amelia would have liked to say, "You may return my sister," but she bit her tongue and allowed Sir Richard to make the introductions.

Mr. Chicore held out both hands to her, saying, "I am so pleased that you have called, Miss Grant. Clarisse feared you would cut her off forever."

He hurried out from behind the counter, rushed past her to the door, opened it, and, bowing, said, "Please do accompany me to our home. Your presence will relieve my dear wife's mind."

Amelia remembered her resolve and stammered, "I—you—you must not think that my presence designates my approval, Mr. Chicore. It is quite beyond my understanding how you could have done such an evil thing."

Mr. Chicore stopped, drew his eyebrows together in true dismay, and said, "Miss Grant, despise me forever. I deserve it. But please forgive Clarisse. Our only crime is that we loved each other and could not bear to be parted."

"One does not encourage a young woman to run off from her family, despite love," Amelia said.

"Had I come to you and made offer for Clarisse, would you have agreed?" he asked.

"No," Amelia said.

"Then what was I to do?" he asked. "But please, before you quite dismiss me, come see Clarisse."

As that had been her intention from the first, Amelia followed him. They walked a short distance past shops, turned into a cobbled lane, and then, to her relief, entered a deep garden, tree shaded and neatly hedged. The house reminded her of their old home at Pickerton Cross, with mullioned windows and a full second story. A housemaid opened the door for them.

Before Amelia could remove her bonnet, Clarisse flew down the stairs and into her arms, crying, "Amelia! Oh, Amelia, how good of you!"

And to Amelia's amazed annoyance, she discovered that it was far easier to accept the description of "good" than start a pointless criticism. Worse, there was nought to criticize. Clarisse wore a new and lovely muslin of a creamy shade, embroidered with roses that matched her cheeks. Her eyes glowed. Her golden curls tumbled about her shoulders.

"You are quite happy?" Amelia asked.

Clarisse laughed, caught her hand, and dragged her through the house, showing her how spacious and well furnished it was.

As Amelia admitted to Sir Richard on their journey home, "Mr. Chicore may be but a tradesman, yet he seems a prosperous one. Did you know this before we saw his shop and home?"

Sir Richard nodded. "I knew. I queried on receipt

of my grandmother's message. He is very comfortably off."

"Had it not been so, had Clarisse been living in a room above some small, poor shop, would you have taken me there?"

"Not so quickly," he admitted.

"It was kind of you. Yet, one wishes Clarisse had been less disposed to Mr. Chicore."

"You did not like him, then?"

"I liked him well enough," Amelia said. "He seems most pleasant and it is quite apparent he treats Clarisse well. It is only—only I wished more for her."

"What did you wish?"

Amelia peered up at him from beneath her bonnet rim. The late afternoon sun shone through the carriage window, turning his light-brown hair to bronze and outlining his thin, handsome face. She was sure she should not confide in him, yet he had been so thoughtful that at times she found herself regarding him as a family member. And she did need someone of knowledge with whom to speak.

"I—I wished her to at least marry a member of the—that is, I wish Mr. Chicore were of our own kind. Not that he is not good enough, not that, but tradespeople—ah—their fortunes can so quickly be lost."

"A reasonable worry. Had you someone else in mind for Clarisse?"

How had he cut so quickly to the heart of her thoughts? Amelia said carefully, "I had rather—that is, it did seem to me that—I rather thought Lord Pendarvin. He often comes to call." Then she added in an embarrassed rush, "I know Clarisse is not clever, but she is very pretty, and I did think that with a bit of time and some social practice at Aunt Sophie's home she might—oh, you see, none of it matters now."

Was he laughing at her? His face remained solemn but his eyes sparkled. "Did his lordship display an interest?"

"How can I tell! And as for that, I have rather changed my mind. I think him quite too well off. That is, once I might have thought, but now—oh, things have changed."

"I cannot follow your meaning," he said.

Amelia's anger flamed her cheeks. She spoke carefully, separating her words, sorting her thoughts. "I must tell you truthfully, Sir Richard, that the month I spent at Mandeville Hall has changed my thoughts of the titled, with their country houses and their stables and their most improper parties and behavior and oh!"

She clamped her hand over her mouth.

He leaned back in the carriage and chuckled softly. Then he gently took her hand in his and said, "Dear Amelia Grant, I can understand your misgivings. Had I known you were to take that position at Mandeville Hall, I would have interfered. Your Aunt Sophie knows the Mandevilles only vaguely, never having attended their home or their parties."

"Then you have attended their parties?"

"On occasion," he said.

Amelia drew her hand from his and carefully folded her hands together in her lap. She could not imagine the meaning of his gesture, but she thought it meant as a brotherly sort of comfort and did not want to offend him. Yet if he were of such behavior as the guests at the rout-party, she must once and finally dismiss him from her ambitions for Berdine.

"Are all country parties like those at Mandeville Hall?" she asked without looking at him.

"They vary. I think it safe to say that few hostesses are equal to Lady Mandeville."

Amelia remembered her ladyship racing across the countryside in her rose silk ballgown, her black hair streaming loose in the moonlight. "No, I should think not. But are all guests of such behavior?"

"Of what behavior?"

Did he mock her? She could not possibly ask if all guests at rout-parties imbibed heavily and made indecent advances to unwilling females. Ignoring his question, she stared out the window and continued the journey in silence. When they arrived at Puddleafton, she thanked him kindly but did not invite him in. She must, she decided, look further for a husband for Berdine. Somewhere, surely, existed a gentleman of means who also possessed decorum and a conservative nature.

With these thoughts in mind she did not find undesirable a call from Lord Pendarvin the following day. He had always struck her as gentler, shyer, and far better suited for marriage than Sir Richard. She could not imagine him as a guest at one of the Mandeville Hall parties. When she ventured to question him on this point, he sounded astonished.

"Mandeville Hall! No, I have never attended a do there. Not even called in! It is—uh—rather out of my way. Of course, I have met the Mandevilles."

"The parties," Amelia murmured, as she led him around the house to point out the kitchen garden, "are unusual. At least, I suppose they are. I have nothing with which to compare them except the balls at Bath."

"Less do-about, I'd wager."

"Much less formal. And a bit—ah—noisier."

"Oh?"

"It is difficult to say."

"It is? You always seem to me a quick one with a right word and a good eye for judging, Miss Grant. I am no authority on parties, mind, as I don't attend except when my mother commands—well—I'm not much for the dance."

"Do you not?" she asked.

He leaned over a garden row, running the leaves of the tattie plants through his fingers, examining their small, flowering stalks. If one judged him from his expression of intent fascination, one might think him a gardener. But then, of course, one would have to ignore the superb cut of his crisp black hair, his perfect features, and his expensive coat and boots. True, though both were of the best quality and cut, the coat was rumpled and the boots mud spattered. She could well imagine him as the cause of great despair to his valet.

He smiled up at her, his dark eyes sparkling, then resumed his study of the carrot rows as he talked. "I am sure I must have told you so. My mother insists that the first words I say to any female are 'I do not care for dancing'; but I hope she exaggerates."

"I do recall you saying so, but Sir Richard assured me that you jested."

"So he would," he said. "Wyland is not to be trusted, ma'am. Still, if you're puzzled about parties, he'd be top-know! Can't be a London hostess who doesn't dote on Wyland."

"Truly? Why should that be so?"

The viscount stood up and looked down at her, his face solemn. "He can be counted on to stand up with every lady. Don't matter her age or looks, he's never short on fancy speeches."

"Do you not like him, then?" Amelia asked.

"Like him? Of course I like him! Salt of the earth, is Wyland. But you didn't ask me about his character, for which I'd vouch any time, but of his turn-out at parties. I wish I had his style. I don't half like parties, but my position—that is, I have to attend a few. Well, in truth, it's not so much my position as my mother."

Amelia laughed, saying, "I am sure she thinks only of your welfare."

"She does," he agreed. "Pity we don't share views on what best suits me."

"Perhaps," Amelia ventured, a new idea growing in her mind, "it is the consumption of spirits at entertainments that you do not care for. Or perhaps you dislike the gaming."

"No," he said. "It's the dancing. I do not like the dance."

Amelia wished there were another way to word her question and learn if he overimbibed or was a gambler, but she could think of none. If she were sure he had neither of these traits, she might still consider him as a suitable husband for Berdine. True, that took a minor adjustment in her outlook, as she had pictured him with Clarisse, but such changes could be made if he proved unlike the Mandevilles. She had been tempted to eliminate the social set from her sister's life, doubting that Berdine could find happiness in surroundings that bore any resemblance to

Mandeville Hall, but now she wondered if that had been too hasty a conclusion. No one could be less like the Mandevilles than the soft-voiced viscount.

"I—I found the consumption of spirits in somewhat indiscriminate quantity to be quite unacceptable," Amelia offered, adding, "That is, I do not presume to criticize the Mandevilles. It is just that I found it confusing."

"I should think you might!" he exclaimed. "What can they have been thinking of, to expose you to such. Indeed, Miss Grant, when such befell, you should have sent word to me. I would have come to your rescue at once."

"I was not in any danger. That is, I was only surprised. I—my father did not use spirits to any degree."

"You had every right to be offended," he said. "Now that you mention it, I rather fancy I have heard tell of their parties. As I do not care for any parties, I am no authority, but I suspect theirs are somewhat more—um, less—ah—more—"

"Wild than most?" Amelia suggested.

He nodded solemn agreement.

Perhaps, after all, he would do for Berdine.

Having made this decision, Amelia decided that her next logical step would be to inform Berdine. She had made a grave error in not speaking firmly to Clarisse about the possibility of marriage to Lord Pendarvin. She should have done so before Clarisse went off to Ireland so that Clarisse would have had his lordship's memory firmly in her mind and heart. That might have protected her from succumbing to the charms of Mr. Edmond Chicore. Amelia determined not to make a like error with Berdine.

That very afternoon she sat Berdine down firmly in the chair in the bedchamber, perched herself on the bed's edge, and said, "Berdine, I have come to definite conclusions about your future."

Berdine folded her hands in her lap, smiled gently, and said, "I am sure you know best, Amelia."

"As is apparent, our enrollment has dropped to a level where it is impossible to maintain ourselves. Although I had hoped that we would not feel so pressed, I fear that we must proceed with my original intentions with some haste."

Berdine blinked but said nothing.

"Dear, you do recall that I originally planned to first introduce Clarisse to Bath society, with the hope of finding her a suitable marriage, and after that, I would do the same for you."

"Yes," Berdine said. "I am relieved that Clarisse is happy in her marriage and that you have seen her."

"Her marriage may prove satisfactory for her, but I fear it does not aid us."

"What is that, Amelia?"

Amelia chewed her lip, sorting her thoughts. She knew well enough what she wished to say but she also knew that she must say it in just the correct manner or Berdine would find it offensive. She would do as bidden, but she would not approve. Amelia did not want sorrowful obedience.

"It is this way," Amelia said. "While Mr. Chicore is wealthy enough to care for Clarisse, he has no social connections. Her marriage to him does not provide desirable introductions to eligible gentlemen for you. Nor can he, in future, benefit Daphne. Therefore, it is most important that your marriage be to a gentleman of—of prospect."

"Prospect?" Berdine asked.

"I have put it badly. What I mean to say is that he must have promise."

Berdine shook her head in confusion.

Out of patience, Amelia exclaimed, "It is quite simple, Berdine! If you were to marry Lord Pendarvin, he could not only provide suitable suitors for Daphne, he might even make a marriage settlement on her. He is very kindhearted and I think has an affection for her."

"Lord Pendarvin!" Berdine leaned back in the chair, her face suddenly pale.

"Do you not care for him?" Amelia asked. "He is most pleasant, very gentle, and I think he has a true regard for you. Of course, he has not yet spoken, but with any encouragement, I believe he will. I also believe his mother is anxious for him to marry, from hints he has dropped."

"Marry him? Amelia, I could not!"

"Well, I do not mean to rush you," Amelia said. "Certainly he will not offer tomorrow. But if Aunt Sophie and myself can put the two of you in each other's company throughout the summer—"

"No," Berdine whispered.

"Is he so repulsive to you?" Amelia asked.

"He is—he is a very admirable gentleman and I respect and—oh, Amelia—it is impossible!" Berdine gasped. She clasped her handkerchief to her face, jumped up, and ran from the room.

"What possesses her?" Amelia muttered. Then she sank back on the bed, let her body relax, and ignored possible wrinkles to her gown. Staring at the ceiling, she tried to sort out Berdine's behavior.

Perhaps it was not too complex, after all. She was

very young in many ways, though in years she was older than Clarisse and Daphne. She had about her an innocence that all mothers seemed to wish in their daughters and which few daughters possessed. The thought of marriage, with its intimacy, no doubt frightened her. It rather flustered Amelia, when she considered it and was truthful with herself.

What Berdine needed was time. Amelia would go tomorrow to Aunt Sophie. They would plan out a series of meetings between Berdine and his lordship. They would not allow the viscount to hurry Berdine, though it was hard to imagine him hurrying anyone. Even if he offered for Berdine, Amelia would assure him of the eventual outcome while directing him to wait until the proper time before informing Berdine of his wishes.

Yes, of course, that was all that was needed. Time. When Berdine knew him well, her fears would disappear. She was by nature affectionate and loving. If she once grew to love the viscount, she would then want to become a part of his life, the better to protect and cherish him from the sins of a wicked world.

Amelia smiled at the ceiling. That was the way she would explain it to Berdine. "My dearest," she would say, "the viscount is an extremely eligible man, rich, sweet, charming, and such young men attract the wicked who would take advantage of them and lead them astray. He needs the protection of a strong, pious woman who will cherish him and guide his soul toward salvation."

It was a nice speech. Unfortunately, Amelia did not have the opportunity to present it.

The very next afternoon, after the children were dismissed and Berdine and Daphne had left for the shops, the curate called. He stood stiffly so that his height matched hers. His gaze was unswerving. She could not draw away her own eyes. It startled her, as she had thought him a very boyish gentleman with his soft face and slightly upturned nose.

He refused her offer of tea and remained firmly in the schoolroom. Amelia had not even had time to remove her apron.

"This is perhaps not the way I had intended to approach you, Miss Grant," he said, "but it seems that situations alter. Berdine has informed me that you have begun to make plans to arrange a marriage for her."

Amelia tried not to show her surprise. She was not unaware that some attraction existed between the curate and Berdine, but she had hardly supposed it open enough to allow him to interfere in a family matter. And why had Berdine confided in the curate?

When Amelia said nothing, Mr. Measure said, "Miss Grant, I do know that I have nought to offer. I realize that, with her family background, Berdine is a young lady of expectations; yet in truth, I think she does not wish to accept your choice of husband."

"I am puzzled, Mr. Measure, as to how this matter is of concern to you. Or why Berdine should have reported such news to you. Did she ask that you speak to me?"

"Rather, she came weeping to find me," he admitted, and for the first time, his gaze wavered. "It is quite possible that if you insist, she will do your bidding. She is most obedient and sensitive to her obligations."

"Mr. Measure, I have no intention of forcing my sister to marry sooner than she may wish or to anyone whom she finds distasteful," Amelia said. "Your concern is a reflection of your kindness, I am sure, but the matter does truly lie within the family and I should prefer it to remain there."

"I fear that is not possible," he said. "Now that the issue has been aired, it is only a fairness to you to fully inform you of the difficulty of the matter. You see—I hesitate to cause you any unhappiness, Miss Grant, but I must speak the truth. Berdine and I—that is—Miss Grant, I know I have nought to offer but myself and my position of respectability, yet I must make bold to offer for Berdine."

"Offer for—but she does not wish to marry at all!" Amelia gasped.

"If that is so, I do withdraw my offer. I wish only for her happiness. But let me say that I am persuaded that Berdine will accept no other offer, because she wishes to accept mine."

"Then you have spoken to her of this?" Amelia asked.

"I—we—Miss Grant, I have for you the fondest admiration. I understand the sacrifices you have made to provide care for your family. I could not come between you and your sister, so I will assure you that if you do not approve of me as a husband for Berdine, I shall press no further."

That he was not an Edmond Chicore, Amelia knew. It was not only his position in the church that guaranteed his word. Mr. John Measure was a man of such devout adherence to duty that he, like Berdine, would never break with convention merely to satisfy his own wishes. The thought crossed Amelia's mind that such an attitude promised a good deal of boredom in one's life, but she brushed that aside. Did she not strive for just such behavior in herself? Yes, but she did not succeed to the degree of Mr. Measure or Berdine. Constantly she bent convention and had done so from the time she had realized she must take over the control of the family's income from her father.

Had she followed all the acceptable standards of behavior, she would have allowed her father to ruin them, as did many an obedient daughter. Then she would have thrown herself on the mercy of her great-aunt, sought refuge in her home, and allowed that kind relative either to find husbands for herself and her sisters or to retire them all off to some upper chamber in her country estate. When Aunt Sophie passed on and her estate fell into the hands of her nephew and heir, any unmarried Grants would then become part of a legion of unwanted spinsters, tucked away in back rooms or country cottages, forced constantly to pretend adoration and gratitude for crumbs cast by a resentful male relative.

It was because she knew where fate could lead that she had turned a stiffened jaw to convention, taken charge of her family, and now intended, no matter what the personal suffering, to create a living that would let them escape dependency. If in so doing she found a few glimmers of pleasure, such as she had felt when paid her first tuition or when the coachman gave her the coins from Sir Archdrake, she hoped she had not become so prideful as to frown down on those who remained tied to convention.

All these troubling ideas confused Amelia long after she had bade Mr. Measure a good day, assuring him that she would take his words into consideration before deciding Berdine's future. No wonder that when Berdine returned, she found Amelia still seated at the desk in the schoolroom, chin in hands, frowning.

"Amelia?" she said softly. "Are you feeling unwell?"

"No, dear. Come here, Berdine, I think we must speak further."

Berdine paled but sank obediently into one of the small classroom chairs.

"Berdine, was there some special reason why you spoke to Mr. Measure of my suggestion that you consider marriage to the viscount?"

Berdine's small round face flushed a deep red. Even though she had only just removed her bonnet, Amelia noticed that her hair lay smooth, not a wisp pulling loose, pulled back into its neat, dark brown knot. Her muslin dress showed not a wrinkle or chalk smear, though she had worn it all day. Her hands, folded before her on the small table, were that lovely white only maintained by ladies who always remembered to wear their gloves out of doors in all weathers.

Berdine said softly, "He is my spiritual guide. I did think it appropriate. Was it not?"

"Is that the only reason?"

Berdine looked up, her brown eyes troubled. "Did he speak to you today?"

"Yes."

"What—what did he say?"

"He made some rather startling comments. That is, they were startling to me. They may be of no surprise for you."

Now it was Berdine who waited, unable to ask further.

Amelia relented. It was all very well for her to head the family, but in truth, there was no way that she could maintain the aloof propriety of a male parent. "Berdine, he offered for you. Did you know he would?"

If it was possible for a deep blush to deepen, Berdine's did. She could not speak.

"Then you and he have spoken of marriage?"

Berdine pressed her lips tightly. Amelia waited. Slowly Berdine said, "Amelia, I would do anything to please you. You have been so good to me. I cannot bear to distress you."

"But you wish to marry Mr. Measure," Amelia said flatly.

"I—I had no intention—that is, at first I was attracted only by his deep reverence and his wide knowledge of religious subjects. When I was troubled by any passage in my Bible, I found him able to clarify it beautifully."

"He is a poor man, Berdine. He will always be poor."

"I care not for that! You know that worldly possessions do not concern me."

That was true. Of them all, Berdine was most satisfied to wear last year's gown, as well she might be, for be it last year's or this year's or next year's, always it would be of a mouse gray or dull brown and decorated with a simple ribbon, never more. She tolerated Clarisse's endless tatted flounces with good humor only because Clarisse made them, not because she really cared for them on her nightdresses and undergarments and bed linens. When Amelia had divided between them her mother's jewelry, Berdine had accepted Mother's locket with tear-filled eyes, yet she never wore it. She kept it wrapped in silk by her Bible, loving it for its memories rather than for its decorative value.

Indeed, what happiness would she find in a grand house filled with ornate furnishings and servants, called upon to hostess lavish banquets and travel to London and Bath for the Seasons? Why had Amelia ever dreamed any of this would interest Berdine?

She said, "Berdine, my darling, listen to me. You need not marry at all if you do not wish it. Together we shall build our school and quietly maintain ourselves. But I must know this. What is it most in your heart to do? Do you wish to accept Mr. Measure's offer? Would you be happy with him?"

Amelia knew, as soon as she asked, how blind she had been. Would Berdine stretch the rules of her upbringing by sending Daphne to the shops so that she could be alone with Mr. Measure for a few moments if she were not in love with him? Even the most pressing religious problem would hardly have tempted her to do so.

Berdine's eyes shone. "Oh, yes," she whispered. "I would be happy."

CHAPTER 16

And she was. Amelia had never seen such a happy bride. Even beautiful Clarisse, who came with Mr. Chicore to attend the marriage ceremony, was totally outshone by the little bride. To add to her joy Aunt Sophie provided a settlement, allowing Berdine to enter proudly into her marriage.

"I find it quite shocking that both of the girls have married so badly," Aunt Sophie confided in Amelia, "yet at least I can do this small thing. I shall do likewise for Clarisse, but I shall not give it to her now or it would only become part of Mr. Chicore's wealth. Rather, I shall have the sum put aside against the day she is widowed."

Amelia laughed. "Aunt Sophie, he is really not bad. I must admit that as I know Mr. Chicore better, I grow fond of him."

"Hmmph, charm enough, I suppose, and seems well intentioned toward our Clarisse, but that hardly displaces the lack of breeding," Aunt Sophie said.

Aunt Sophie had stopped by the cottage a week after the wedding, sweeping through the garden in her ruffled lavender silk gown. Amelia had helped her remove her marvelous mauve bonnet with its blossomings of ribbon and lace. Then she had settled

Aunt Sophie in a chair in the dining room, tucking pillows in about her.

"Stop your fussing, Amelia," Aunt Sophie complained. "Tell me, have you seen our new Mrs. Measure today?"

"She stops by daily," Amelia said. "She was so pleased that you attended her marriage. And she is so happy, Aunt Sophie. Though I might have wished her wealthier, I could not wish her happier. They are truly suited."

"Sentimental twaddle," Aunt Sophie said. Her round face was still flushed beneath its powder from the effort of walking into the house. Her halo of powdered hair slid over her forehead. Her scent filled the room, a scent that matched her lavender dress with its pungent, flowery lightness.

"She insists on helping me," Amelia said, "though I have assured her she need not. Poor Berdine. No matter what her joys, guilt will ever be with her. She thinks she is obligated to continue teaching, especially now that our enrollment has again risen. Indeed, I think she is responsible for that. Many parents seem to think that a wife of the curate must be a suitable educator for their young."

What Amelia did not say was that Berdine's marriage to the curate had apparently offset any gossip started by the marchioness.

"That is all well enough," Aunt Sophie snapped, "but it does not insure a life of leisure for you and Daphne."

"But Aunt Sophie, I thought you were the one who so admired Mrs. Wollstonecraft's independence, yet certainly she lacked affluence." Amelia had touched on the subject to turn Aunt Sophie's thoughts, as she well knew.

Aunt Sophie leaned back into the pillows, her powdered cheeks creased by her smile, her mind drifting to years past. "I do remember her," she said. "I was so honored to meet her. It was at one of Mr. Johnson's little dinners. Not the one from Bath, he was an impossible man! No, it was the printer, the one who published her writings, such a clever man, and there she was. She'd walked alone, did it every day, to take dinner with him. Right through some of the least desirable areas of London, she'd come alone, never worried, never bothered, or if she worried, she never let anyone know. I did so admire her."

"Yet she wasn't rich," Amelia said.

"She was, indeed," Aunt Sophie said. "She had her mind, so she didn't need an inheritance. She had her mind and she knew how to use it. Never knew another like her, though they say her daughter is clever."

"They say a good many things about her daughter," Amelia said, then put her hand over her mouth, wishing she could take back her words. Daphne repeated such a variety of tattle, even tales of Mary Wollstonecraft's daughter, and how the gossips of Puddleafton heard such stories was beyond Amelia's guessing.

"Clever, too, I'll be bound," Aunt Sophie said smoothly, "and they say she has her mother's talent with the pen. Mark me, Amelia, if it's true, she'll have her fame."

Amelia said, "Nonetheless, as I have no talent, I must make do with industry. I had hoped that either

Clarisse or Berdine would marry gentlemen who could provide homes for Daphne, but as this is not the case, I will be frank with you, Aunt Sophie, and tell you that I hope you will be willing to extend your care to her when she is a bit older so that she, at least, will make a suitable marriage."

"She may come live with me now," Aunt Sophie said.

"She won't do that," Amelia said. "I will admit that I have suggested it, thinking that if she resided with you now, by her eighteenth year she would well be suited to be presented. Unfortunately, she is more stubborn than all of us and will not leave Puddleafton."

"She is so fond of this village?" Aunt Sophie asked, surprised.

"She really is. Unfortunately, she knows everyone, even those whom she should not and could not have met properly, I fear. And then there is her garden. She quite adores it."

"Certainly Daphne is welcome to a corner of my property on which to plan whatever garden she might desire," Aunt Sophie said. "She could oversee a staff of gardeners, should she so desire."

"That is not quite what she desires," Amelia said, and sighed, thinking of Daphne with her skirts tucked up, her boot pressing on her spade, her hands and face dirt-streaked.

"What we must do, Amelia, is begin immediately to bend the twig. I shall invite you and Daphne to join me at least twice a week. No, no, it is no bother. I will send my carriage for you. And I shall arrange that suitable company be present. I shall have my modiste make correct gowns. We shall overwhelm

Daphne with charming gentlemen so that her thoughts will be towards those who are acceptable as husbands for Stafford women. There, not another word!"

"That's very kind," Amelia said.

"I shall rather like it," Aunt Sophie said. Then, in a rustling of silk, she leaned forward and asked, "But we do not overlook some facet—ah, not to put too fine a point, but, Amelia, might Daphne have a talent? Might she, ah, have a gift for composition?"

Amelia laughed. "I am afraid that although Daphne may well have Mary Wollstonecraft's independence of spirit, she lacks her talent. Daphne's only outstanding gift is her ability to make plants leap up from the very ground she touches. And I rather suspect there is little future wealth available to female gardeners."

Aunt Sophie shrugged her plump shoulders. "It is a gift best left unmentioned. You are right, Amelia, we must polish her up and settle her with a wealthy marriage."

All very well, Amelia decided after Aunt Sophie had gone, to think to settle Daphne suitably, but one must consider Daphne. She was not a pan of dough to be rapped sharply on a table edge to force it to settle evenly around the rim. She had her own mind, and a very strong mind it was. And as for marriage, she was, after all, but fourteen.

In the meanwhile Amelia concluded she had better bend her energies toward managing her school and earning enough money to keep them out of debt. She had written to Father of the marriages of Berdine and Clarisse and been surprised and gratified to receive an answer. It was his first letter to her in her

lifetime. That it consisted of no more than three
sentences was not to detract from the effort spent in
its writing. She could see the effort and realized, from
the cross-outs and misspellings and omitted words,
that his mind was dimming with age.

> Dear Amelia, I am pleased to hear that Ber-
> dine and Clarisse are married and happy. My
> good friend and cousin cares well for me. Give
> my kindest affections to your sisters and your-
> self. Your father.

Amelia put away her guilt as she put away his
letter. If it were possible, she would journey to Wales
to ascertain his security and offer him a home with
herself and Daphne. But it was not possible. Perhaps
in another year their finances would allow her to
accept again the responsibility of her father.

"I cannot see why you worry," Daphne said. "He
is quite well off and satisfied with himself."

"Do you believe so?"

"If he were not, he would be on our doorstep."

"I suppose you are right," Amelia conceded.

Father had always done as he pleased. She had
presumed that was because he was a male. But she
was learning otherwise. It was more than his sex that
determined his nature. It was obviously an inherited
trait. It had passed down through the Grant line and
landed heavily in Daphne. Try as she might, Amelia
could not persuade, trick, or tempt Daphne toward
the course that Aunt Sophie had sensibly suggested
for her.

"No," Daphne said, when Amelia told her that
Aunt Sophie's modiste would cut gowns for them.

"Save her the trip, Amelia, unless you fancy new finery for yourself. Berdine has made up three frocks for me now and they suit me perfectly and are all I need."

The frocks Berdine had made, at Daphne's instruction, were sturdy cotton, one a dark red, one a dark green, and one in a sprigged pattern of dark-blue flowers on a light-blue background. They fit perfectly but a bit loosely, meeting Berdine's standards of modesty and Daphne's wish for frocks in which she could move easily. They had no ruffles, embroidery, tatting, or lace.

"Trimmings forever tear," Daphne had told Berdine. Although Berdine thought that a bit of trimming that could tear worked well to encourage grace in a female, she also believed that trimming might possibly be a form of vanity. Torn between religious doubts and Daphne's stubbornness, Berdine forewent the trimmings. Instead she lavished them on Anne's gowns. Certainly the angels themselves must understand that an orphaned child needed special luxuries, she confided to Amelia.

Amelia quite enjoyed seeing young Anne Measure blossom under Berdine's care, her hair now brushed to shining, her frocks well cared for, her thin face widening more often into a shy smile.

But Daphne was another concern completely. She had blossomed quite enough. She was tall, thin, broad shouldered, and had long, narrow hands and feet. Despite her unfashionable features, she was extremely beautiful, with eyes the color of the summer sky, lashes that curled dark and silky, hair like sunshine. Her features were stronger than those of Clarisse, the nose slightly larger and well sculpted to a straight, slender line, the jaw squared and firm. Her complexion had the texture of a rose petal. To Berdine's displeasure, it had not a rose color. It glowed a golden brown and freckles shone like sun flecks across her nose.

"She looks more like a milkmaid each day," Berdine sighed.

In the end it made little difference how Daphne looked. She not only refused the silk and fragile muslin gowns offered by Aunt Sophie, describing them as absurd and useless, but she also refused to waste time visiting Aunt Sophie during calling hours, when Aunt Sophie's friends were there.

She said firmly, "I love Aunt Sophie and shall be most delighted to visit her any morning when we may speak together, but I shall not sit in the drawing room on those ridiculous, small chairs balancing teacups and wasting time on foolish chatter with dandies."

"Dandies! I do not like that word," Amelia complained.

"Call them what you will," Daphne shrugged. "They are useless people who have nothing better to do than change their clothes five times a day. I cannot be bothered."

"But you must learn to present yourself correctly," Amelia said.

Daphne flashed a mischievous grin. "Am I to be made tempting in hopes of an offer from some rich and titled muttonhead?"

"You are but fourteen! Indeed not!"

"Yet that is your future hope. Dear Amelia, I do not think you will gain much by attempting to mold me into a fine lady. I cannot imagine myself settled in a marriage. Like you, I much prefer to live my own way, with no silly male to dominate me."

"Daphne! That is not my reason at all," Amelia protested.

"Oh, I know you tell yourself that you do not wed because your obligations to your family prevent it. It is a convenient excuse. In truth, I do not think you care to wed."

Amelia stamped her foot. "Let me tell you this, dear sister. At this moment I should be quite grateful for a husband to whom I could give my responsibility for you and my father. However, I cannot believe such a bravehearted male exists."

"Quite correct. Though there may be a male who could manage Father, there is none who could manage me. With that understood between us, I shall return to my garden and you may send word to Aunt Sophie that I have no need of her modiste."

And that was the last Daphne would speak on the subject.

Amelia's only consolation was that Daphne was young and might well change her mind if left alone and allowed to mature. She herself had not, at fourteen, had any interest in gentlemen. For that matter, she told herself severely, she had none now. If the face of a certain gentleman occasionally intruded on her dreams, it was only that he made himself present so often that she almost regarded him as a family member.

Indeed, two gentlemen could well have been family members, from the frequency of their calls. Amelia did not discourage them, recognizing them both as charming and hoping some of that charm would lure Daphne toward a more genteel behavior. It was unfortunate that both gentlemen seemed to enjoy Daphne as she was, never raising eyebrows, constantly visiting with her about her garden.

At last, in exasperation, Amelia told the viscount, "I do wish you would do less to encourage Daphne in her ways. Could you not mention to her how pleasant it is to engage in social entertainments?"

His face remained serious but his dark eyes twinkled with amusement. They sat together on a bench at the back of the kitchen garden, where a half circle of hollyhocks created a colorful and private nook. It was late August, the sunlight streamed down onto Amelia's parasol, and the vegetables spilled over in their rows. Brilliant flowers bordered the beds and paths. Butterflies darted from petal to petal. The kitchen cats lazed on the back step, the black soundly asleep, the gray with one eye half-open to watch a bird hop along the fence pickets.

Young Pendarvin said, "I can't hoax her that I'm mad for dances. Truth is, I can't abide them."

"But you could tell her of banquets and hunt parties and musicales and the theater and, oh, you know better than I!"

"Is that the life you'd wish for?" he asked softly.

"How can I know? I have no time for such," Amelia said, although she thought privately that such an empty existence would soon bore her. The yellow silk parasol created a bright, sunrise frame. She looked like a portrait in her pale muslin. Her eyes were dark with worry, making them look even larger in her soft face. A silky curl slipped loose from its ribbon to shadow her brow.

"Would it please you to have time for such?" he persisted.

"I do not complain of my lot," she said, almost wishing she had not begun the subject. She could not think how their words had switched from Daphne to herself. "It is only that I want so much more for Daphne, a life of security and ease."

"But what of you? Would you like that sort of life?"

She said firmly, "I cannot waste my thoughts on my own comforts when I have my sister and father as my responsibilities."

"Shouldn't think you need do. Shouldn't think it at all. Why not spread it out a bit?"

"I cannot ignore my duty," she said. "Clarisse is comfortably off, but not enough to accept the financial burden of either of them, and I fear the Measures can scarcely afford themselves."

"Not what I had in mind," he said softly. While the toe of his boot traced a circle in the earth, he continued slowly, "Haven't got Wyland's charming speech, I know, but I'd best push on with what I have to say. Hope you won't misunderstand. It—it seems to me that if you would allow it—that is, I—I could cut your troubles. Shoulder them. Take them over. Be my pleasure to do so, Miss Grant—Amelia. Thought I—I'd not rush you into any decision."

Amelia stared at him and almost dropped her parasol.

"I—I hope I've not offended you," he said, meeting her startled gaze.

"Lord Pendarvin! Would you—that is, I don't—"

"I have said it badly. Knew I would! I've no experience in this! Lord, I don't suppose a man admits that, though. Thing is, I never before met a lady to whom I wished to make an offer."

"Then you are proposing!" Amelia exclaimed.

"Yes, I am." He watched her. When she said nothing more, he continued slowly, "You must know I've no shortage of brass. Makes me free to marry whom I please. I'd—it would give me great—I'd like to provide for you, Amelia, and for Daphne, too, of course. Don't mean it as a brag, but my estate is more than large. Plenty of space for Daphne. She could have all she fancied for her garden. Run the whole thing, for all I'd mind. Or if you'd rather, I could set a sum on her. She could be a—what's the word—a woman of independent means. As for your father, that's no worry. I've always had gaming uncles to settle up for. He'd only be one more."

"How efficient you are," Amelia managed to say, her voice shaking with nervousness as she could not quite bring herself to give him an answer. He was so exceedingly kind.

"It's all I am. And not always that," he said, scowling at his boot toe. "Can't dance or write love poems."

"I should not think either quality necessary in a husband," Amelia said.

A smile turned his handsome face into a vision of charm and Amelia could not imagine why, though she truly liked him, she could feel no desire to share her life with him.

"Are—would you—will you have me?"

Amelia chewed her lip, then said slowly, "You are the kindest, most thoughtful person I have ever known. It does seem to me that there must be hundreds of young ladies who have set their caps for you."

"Hundreds! Miss Grant! Oh, you're funning me.

Ah—well, there may be a few. Attracted to my brass or title."

"You are too modest."

He flashed another smile, saying, "My mother'd say otherwise. She's anxious for me to marry. But until I met you—that is—the others—Amelia, I wish you'd say the word." He caught her two slim hands in his broad ones and blurted, "I'm sure we'd suit!"

She did not withdraw her hands. Instead she looked steadily at him and forced herself to speak the truth, though it pained her to hurt him. "My lord—Charles—you are kind and dear! I admire you so much and value your friendship. But I cannot accept you."

To her surprise he did not look particularly hurt, but rather puzzled, and then his brow smoothed and he said, "Tied your heart up elsewhere, then?"

And until he said it, Amelia had denied it to herself. She looked away, not wishing him to see the truth in her eyes. "Please. You are kind but I must refuse."

He said softly, "There now, forget I spoke. Didn't intend to put a spoil on the day."

Amelia giggled, then clapped her hands to her mouth, ashamed. "Oh, dear, I am sorry. But it is so silly, thinking an offer of marriage could spoil a day. Indeed, you have paid me such a fine compliment, I shall always cherish it."

"There now, I'm glad of that. You won't mind if I tell my mother that I offered? Please her no end. She'll consider that progress. That way I make two ladies happy, if not myself. Don't think I can do more in one day." He lifted her hand to his lips, brushed it lightly, then set it gently in her lap. With a bow he said his farewell. "Never thought of myself as a marrying man, but I owed it to my parents to try."

"We shall remain friends?" Amelia asked. "I would like that."

"Always," he said solemnly. "And should you change your mind and think you might fancy me, I'm bound to be available."

As she watched him walk away, Amelia could not believe herself. She had never dreamed anyone would offer for her. Yet here a viscount had offered her a title and wealth, a handsome, kind, and good gentleman, and she had refused him. She had turned him down not because she found him unacceptable as a husband, but because she knew there was for her only one man in all the world. Unfortunately, that man had no desire to marry.

As tears welled in her eyes, Amelia began to understand why Clarisse and Berdine had let their hearts rule their heads.

"I wish I fancied Charles. He is so much nicer," she told herself, then had to smile through her tears. Which, she wondered, would be worse? To love a man who would never propose marriage, or to love a man who only proposed to please his mother?

CHAPTER 17

Summer passed. It drifted right on by, despite Aunt Sophie's disapproval. She was so annoyed by Daphne's refusal to attend her at-homes that Amelia almost began to believe that Aunt Sophie would extend the summer season right through to Christmas, waiting for Daphne to change her mind.

"It is too bad of the child," Aunt Sophie complained on a golden September afternoon when Amelia had let Richard persuade her to take a drive to visit her aunt.

The three of them strolled through the gardens, admiring the patterns of color. Aunt Sophie walked very slowly, leaning heavily on Richard's arm, her cane held firmly in her other hand. Her purple bonnet cast her powdered face into a deep shadow. The panels of her lavender silk and net gown trailed behind her, stirring the gravel of the path. Amelia wore a muslin that clung more than she liked, but it had been a gift from Aunt Sophie and she chose it for the visit so that her great-aunt would not think her ungrateful. Quite enough to have Daphne overwhelming the old woman with such behavior. Amelia's muslin was the pale yellow of the late summer daisies, gathered at her elbows and bodice with fluttering lengths of white ribbon and lavishly trimmed with lace. Lace lined the brim of her matching yellow straw. She carried her closed parasol, enjoying the warmth of the sun.

At home in the village she always kept her parasol up on such days rather than receive Berdine's chiding. Then also, she had need to set an example for Daphne. But here she could enjoy the sun and if it darkened her complexion, Berdine and Daphne would think it had done so despite her precautions. A twinge of guilt gnawed at her mind. Was she dishonest to so love the warmth on her skin, yet forever scold Daphne for doing the same?

"I think you must let Daphne age a bit," Sir Richard said. "She is not ready for polishing."

"A girl is never too young to begin to attain accomplishments," Aunt Sophie said. "You are very naughty, Richard, to defend that child."

"I find her delightful as she is," he said.

"Oh, indeed! You would! But what do you know of proper deportment in young women? As you lack the slightest interest in ever marrying again, you cannot possibly know what is required of a female to be eligible."

"I am not as dense as all that!" Richard complained. "One need not be in the market for a team to know how to judge the quality of a horse."

"Are you comparing the choosing of a spouse to the purchasing of an animal?" Aunt Sophie cried. "Oh, you are wicked!"

Richard had the grace to look a bit embarrassed. Amelia tilted her head to gaze at him from beneath her bonnet rim, her eyebrows raised.

"I meant no such thing!" he insisted.

"Then we both misheard you," Amelia said.

He bowed and gave her a wide smile. "Dear, beautiful lady, you have caught me out. I have expressed myself quite badly. It was not my intention at all to compare a lady to an animal, least of all our lovely Daphne. If I would compare her to an animal, however, I would choose something much more graceful. Let me think, perhaps a deer?"

"A deer!" Aunt Sophie cried.

"Indeed, something free and beautiful and untamed."

"I shall agree that she is untamed," Amelia said.

"And Berdine, I think, is the most charming of little brown squirrels."

"What nonsense!" Aunt Sophie said.

As Amelia had often thought of Berdine as a squirrel, she was intrigued. "You seem to have made a woodland of the Grant family. Tell me, Sir Richard, how do you envision Clarisse and myself?"

He pinched his forehead into a deep frown, but Amelia suspected he was playacting to tease her. Finally he said, "Ah, quite clear, dear Miss Grant. The incomparable Mrs. Chicore is a butterfly, *that* butterfly, the one that flutters even now in the roses. But you, Miss Amelia Grant, are more difficult to describe."

"Then, pray, do not try," she said quickly, her heart missing a beat. For as he said her name, she suddenly knew she could not bear to hear his thoughts of her. He would see her as impersonally as he saw her sisters. He would describe her as a bird or kitchen cat or some other silly thing. And she would blush foolishly. And he would guess.

This fear tied her tongue, cast down her eyes, and

caught at her breathing every time she looked at him, until she dreaded his calls. She had only come out with him today because he had said Aunt Sophie was unwell and needed companionship. And also because she was weary of making excuses to him. To all that, had been added Daphne, leaning on her hoe, assuring Sir Richard that while she was much too busy, Amelia was free to go calling.

But despite her protests Richard hurried on with his fanciful chatter, as much to amuse Aunt Sophie as anything, Amelia well knew. Yet she wished she could change the topic to anything else at all.

He said carefully, "I have considered the matter, and now that I am quite convinced that mere words cannot describe Amelia Grant, I shall bravely march ahead. An Englishman may often be a fool, but never a coward. So though my choice is inadequate, Miss Grant, let me say that you are no one object, but rather a complete garden."

"A garden!" Aunt Sophie said. "How quaint of you, Richard."

"Oh yes, I am very quaint. There, see, ladies, the flowers bending in the breeze are Miss Grant's grace. The delphiniums are her eyes, the roses her lips, the tempting shadows beneath the trees are the dark wonder of her hair. And as for her complexion, ah, there we have a problem, for there is not a flower petal in the garden to compare."

Amelia turned her face away from him, studying hard the garden, so that he would not see the tear that rose to burn the corner of her eye. It was all very well for him to have his amusement. It meant nothing to him. To her it was torment. If he meant one word of his ravings, she would be at his feet, sobbing her love.

The thought of such ridiculous behavior, fit only for a silly peagoose or a housemaid, dried the tear. She set her chin firmly and stared straight ahead. The garden, divided into neat, triangular beds edged in clipped yew and separated by gravel walks, spun before her. Each bed shone another blinding color, red, yellow, orange, white, masses of flowers mounding within their low shrub borders.

Her sight faded. Her heartbeat pounded in her ears.

To her considerable surprise she felt Richard's arm about her waist. She tried to move away and could not. She could not even protest.

"I fear she is faint from the sun," she heard him say.

"There, lad, you take her to the house," Aunt Sophie said.

Amelia's mind whirled. She could not believe it. Dizzy spells were not a thing to which she fell subject. Yet it took all her strength to remain on her feet, so that Richard would not pick her up and carry her. She could not even see him now, her vision having dimmed to dark shadows, but she could hear him speaking in her ear.

"Lean on me, Amelia. There, a few more steps, here, love, sit down now."

The spiral of heat that had wound through her body, dulled her brain, and blinded her vision, seemed slowly to withdraw. Her eyes cleared. She sat in dim shadows in the wide entry of Aunt Sophie's manor house, a stiff, carved chair beneath her, a rich oriental carpet at her feet. She looked up slowly and then, unable to prevent it, she shivered violently.

"I have never done such a thing," she whispered.

"Hush," he said gently. "Sit there. You were too long in the sun."

"But Aunt Sophie—"

"She is waiting on a bench. I have sent her maid to fetch her."

"Oh, my," Amelia moaned, "it is she who was ill, not I, and now I have caused her neglect."

"Hush. She is not neglected."

"I do feel so foolish."

"Good, then you must also be feeling improved." From somewhere he produced a shawl and wrapped it around her shoulders. A maid brought a glass of lemonade. Amelia sipped slowly. By the time Aunt Sophie reached the house, supported by her maid, Amelia's brain had stopped its whirl.

"You are looking improved," her aunt said. "Do you think she should stay a few days with me, Richard? The trip back could be tiring."

"It takes but an hour," Amelia protested. "No, no, I am quite well, now, Aunt Sophie. I should have kept my parasol open. Berdine is forever saying so, and I must admit, she is right."

Richard laughed and said, "It is a relief to hear you. I feared you would swoon away."

"I am not the swooning sort," Amelia insisted. "Truly I am not. It was only the sun. But perhaps we should start home now."

"Then you must promise to return in a few days," Aunt Sophie said.

"I—I shall try, Aunt Sophie."

"What do you mean, try?"

"We are so hurried, that is, there is much to do, and oh, I shall return, I promise," she ended weakly. To say otherwise would require an explanation that she did not wish to give.

They took refreshments with Aunt Sophie in her drawing room, so that by the time they started home in Richard's curricle Amelia felt much improved. She chattered about the scenery and Aunt Sophie's garden, about almost anything, in fact, rather than leave spaces in which he could press her for information. She knew from something in his expression that he intended to pursue the business of her faint and she did not want to discuss it. But she could not talk forever. When she ran out, he said, "Now may I speak?"

He sat easily, leaning slightly back, the reins lying loosely across his sun-browned hand, his long legs bent with a relaxed grace, his boots reflecting the sunlight. She avoided his face.

"You do not need my permission to speak," Amelia said.

"Indeed, I do, when you rush to fill each gap with words," he said.

"I must apologize if I cause you boredom," she said.

"You cause me many things, but none of them boredom," he said. "Amelia Grant, you may not care for my interference, but as an old family friend and a lifelong admirer of your aunt, I find myself thinking of you as someone under my protection, though, no, do not interrupt me to protest! I know well that I have no such obligation. It is only that I feel it, rightly or not. And it has come to my notice that you are working far too much at the running of

225

this school. Though I admire your ambition, finding it a charming and unusual trait in a woman, I must say that I think you push it rather too far. I do not think the sun alone disturbed your health today. I think you have grown thinner since first we met, and I thought you rather too thin then."

"That is too much! I must protest! I cannot think my size is your concern!"

"It is when added to it are the shadows beneath your eyes. You are not sleeping enough or eating enough. You are driving yourself with long hours as you would not drive Dora. Do not deny it! I have my sources."

"I can well imagine," Amelia said, and her fingers nervously turned her parasol handle, rolling it over and over where it lay across her knees. "Daphne speaks too freely."

"It matters not where I hear," he said. "What matters is that you have taken on a task meant to be spread among the four sisters, yet now you are left with only Daphne to help you."

"Berdine helps."

"She comes for only an hour each day and will soon stop that," he said.

"That—that is so," Amelia admitted, "but she has not felt well."

"And will feel no better until she is delivered, at which time she will have even more to occupy her in her home than she has now," he said flatly.

"Oh! I had not thought—but even Aunt Sophie has not yet been told," Amelia said. "Oh, my, Daphne must have told you." And to her dismay, she felt her cheeks go red. Really, how could Daphne tell Sir Richard that Berdine was with child, when Berdine had only just realized it herself? Had that child no curb at all to her tongue?

"It is as well she did," he said. "I think you must tell Berdine that you do not need her help. She has only one housekeeper at the parish house, and I think the work there is enough for her."

"I have already told her," Amelia said. What she did not say was that she spent most of her afternoon hours at the parish house now, managing the sewing and keeping the place quiet so that Berdine could rest. And that was why she needed to stay up long after Daphne and Dora had gone to bed, working by candlelight to prepare the next day's lessons.

"You cannot continue this way," he said.

"Really, I have perhaps a summer chill, nothing more, and it is kind of you to concern yourself, Sir Richard, but you must believe I can well manage."

"I do not question your abilities," he said, "only your sensibility."

"My sensibility!"

A warm breeze caught Amelia's bonnet, pulling it away, so that she had to reach up quickly to hold it to her head. He smiled at her and said, "What a charming summer picture you make, Miss Grant."

"Do not bother with such empty flatteries. Tell me what you mean by attacking my sensibility."

"You are not completely honest with yourself or you would admit that you cannot continue at such long hours. You have need of a slower pace, or more help, or perhaps a rest at some seaside haven."

"Very charming, indeed, if one is rich and of the leisured and privileged people. I am not, sir."

"You could be," he said.

Amelia's breath caught. Had Lord Pendarvin told

Sir Richard that he had offered for her hand? Would he be so unkind? Surely he could not—but then, would he consider it unkind or would he mention his offer meaning his mention as a compliment? Certainly it had been a compliment—indeed, the highest a gentleman could pay—yet she wished he had kept it between themselves. Aghast, she said nothing.

"Miss Grant, hear me out. I have thought on your situation, yet I hesitated to speak, knowing your independence and how you value it. But today I have become convinced that you endanger your health and so I shall speak. As you know, I have an estate that encompasses considerable land as well as employing quite a number of families who reside on my lands. I have been disturbed by the inability of the parents to better the minds of their young. I know there are those that believe that servants are best left ignorant, but I do not concur. It would serve me well to provide a school for these children. Some are quite clever. But I must have an educated woman to teach them. And that is where I thought at once of you."

"You want me to run a school on your estate?" Amelia asked, surprised. "I did work a short while as a governess on an estate and I must tell you truthfully that I did not care for it."

"You would be far more than a governess," he said. "You and Daphne would reside in my home as my guests. The school would be cared for by my staff. Your only requirement would be to oversee its running. I could hire as many tutors as you required, so you need not do overmuch."

Live in his house! The thought tore Amelia apart. How could she ever tell him that she would rather die of weariness than live in the same house with him, seeing him day after day, sharing his table, meeting him unexpectedly on the garden paths, passing him constantly in the corridors?

It was impossible. Amelia had firmly lectured herself about the follies of a weak mind that is allowed to be overruled by the heart. More, she knew that any moments of idleness left her mind open to fanciful daydreams, a luxury she could not permit herself. Was it not terrible enough when, aching with exhaustion, she dropped into her bed only to find that instead of sleep, thoughts of Sir Richard haunted her?

"I—I cannot thank you enough for your kindness, Sir Richard. But it is quite impossible."

"Why is it impossible?" he asked.

"I—I must be—I must make my own decisions on these matters. Certainly your offer is generous and inspired by your love for my aunt, this I realize, but nonetheless, we are not related and I could not take advantage of your misplaced concern."

"Neither my love nor my concern is misplaced. I am quite sure that Miss Stafford has no objection to including me in the family."

"No doubt you are right! With no family of her own, she would make Daphne her daughter. And so, I perceive, she thinks of you as a son."

"No," he said firmly, "not a son. Miss Sophie Stafford has never longed for either a husband or children. If she had, she could have had her pick, my dear. No, rather, I think she fancies me as a nephew and I rather fancy her as an aunt."

"Do you?" Amelia asked, relieved to have the conversation turn from herself and the impossible suggestion that she live on his estate.

"One can never have too many relatives. At least, not if they are of the right sort. Certainly one cannot have too many Aunt Sophies."

"How strange. I always think of you as a man who goes his own direction, unencumbered," Amelia said.

"It is my turn to be surprised. What gave you such notion?"

Amelia bit her lip and did not reply. To be cornered into describing him could put her in an awkward position of revealing that she had thought much of him at all.

He pulled the reins lightly and his grays slowed to a walk. "Come along, now, Miss Grant, I insist on a reply."

Fearing that he would stop altogether, she said slowly, "It is only that you move about freely, sometimes here, sometimes London, sometimes Bath, yet you do not take your child with you. You do not— that is, oh, truly, Sir Richard, this is not for me to say. I have no criticism of your way of life. It is quite beyond my concern."

"Ah, you think because I do not travel with a wife and seventeen children, I am not a family man."

"I did not say that."

"And because I do not stay in one place and surround myself with relatives, I am unsettled."

"I said no such thing!" she protested, her blood rising. Turning to glare at him, her arm still raised to keep her bonnet in place, Amelia cried, "It is quite unfair to guess my thoughts. In truth, I know little of you, Sir Richard, other than your kindness to myself and my family. All else can be no more than hearsay and at no time do I deem myself fit to judge you."

To her dismay he laughed at her discomfiture. She had half a mind to tell him her real thoughts, that she knew he was much sought after by London hostesses for his party manners, that he traveled in a society of gamblers and highflyers, that he entertained other men's wives to an extent that she would not want to guess at. Even Aunt Sophie said that he was a permanent bachelor, enjoying a widowhood that had provided him with both an heir and his freedom, the best of choices for such a man.

Could he look into her eyes and read her mind? Amelia turned her face away from him.

"What you have said is quite true," he said. "You do not know me well enough to judge me; therefore how can I expect you to make such a decision? Miss Grant, tomorrow I shall call for you and you must spend a day at my estate. You must see my home and what arrangements and accommodations it could offer you and Daphne before deciding your mind against me."

She shook her head in refusal but he acted as though he had not seen her. He said, "You are too open minded to refuse me a fair showing, are you not?"

She wished she could tell him how unfair that statement was, forcing her to either accompany him or admit that she harbored a prejudice against him. But she feared to say anything. And then he flicked the reins, the horses quickened their pace, and Amelia found herself grabbing her bonnet with both hands. She rearranged it on her head, pulling it forward above her eyes so that it would less catch the wind, and retied the pale-yellow ribbons beneath her stubborn little chin.

"If you are worried that I should be ever at your elbow," he said, "I may relieve you of that fear, Miss Grant. In truth, you are right, I am often elsewhere, so that if you should accept a position with me, you would have as much freedom as you wished."

Would it be worse, wondered Amelia, to bump into him at every turning or to spend weeks mooning over his absence? She recalled well enough her worries during his last trip to London. No, Puddleafton was as close as she wished to live to Sir Richard Wyland. Perhaps it was too close.

CHAPTER 18

As she could find no way to refuse his invitation without becoming involved in long and embarrassing explanations, Amelia accompanied Sir Richard to the Wyland estate for a day of touring the house and grounds.

Wyland Hall rambled pleasantly between oak and chestnut groves, a two-storied gray stone house that had begun as a modest reception hall, library, dining hall, kitchen, and a half dozen bedrooms, then sprouted additions at angles chosen to preserve the large trees. The result was unsymmetrical yet pleasing, keeping the building to its low height and spreading it gently, so that it blended with garden walls, stables, and outbuildings of matching stone, all now overgrown with ivy and rambling roses. Between the blanketing vines the mullioned windows reflected back the morning sun. Behind the buildings low hills lay quietly golden with summer grass and rock outcroppings, dotted with distant sheep flocks. The surrounding grounds, like the Hall itself, had taken their character from extended planning, so that a wide green expanse of lawn stretched down a slope to a shadowed lake that lapped peacefully at the base of its overhanging willow grove.

Sir Richard would not let her walk the paths, warning her against the sun, but instead drove her through the grounds so that she might see the extent of his lands. The flowering shrubs and casual massings of flowers that spilled onto gravel paths gave way, farther from the Hall, to pastures and barns.

Here he stopped his grays and handed Amelia down from her seat.

"I must introduce you to my heart's delight," he said, leading her toward a low stone building surrounded by a waist-high stone wall.

Puzzled, she took his arm. When they reached the wall, she peered over and into two tiny bright eyes in an upturned white face of the largest pig she had ever seen.

"This is my darling Migaloo," he said, and leaned across the wall to scratch the pig's back. "She is the finest sow this side of London."

Amelia giggled.

"Do you question me knowledge of pigs, gel?" he teased.

"No, indeed, I am sure she is all you say and more." Amelia gave the pig thoughtful inspection, then said, "I know nothing of pigs, I must confess, but she is truly handsome."

"There, I knew you were a woman of discernment," he said.

"She is—that is—I thought pigs were less clean."

"You thought the pig yard would have an unpleasant odor," he said. "Let me set you correct on that point. Pigs, my dear, are clean. Pigmen are dirty. All the fault lies there. But for Migaloo I employ the best of pigmen, which is why her pen is clean and she is properly attended."

Next they drove beyond the pastures to a small cluster of cottages. Amelia counted fifteen and was gratified to see them surrounded by kitchen gardens and flower borders, each neater than the other. Children played in the nearby fields. Mothers hung out washing or sat in dooryards shelling peas. All nodded and smiled.

"You provide good homes for your people," Amelia said. She had heard of the conditions in which some farmhands lived and in Pickerton Cross she had often gone with the vicar's wife to help a sick mother and been appalled at conditions in estate cottages.

"I take care of my people and my animals. Indeed, I am a kind and virtuous gentleman," Sir Richard said as they drove back toward the Hall. "Therefore, I cannot see why you hesitate to join my household. The cottagers have among them some forty children. As few of the parents read or write, it would please me extremely to build a school and have their children learn from a proper staff. I know it is unusual. Perhaps you think it beneath you to teach children of such humble background."

"No such thing!" Amelia protested. "It matters not to me a child's background. It is only that—Sir Richard, I do think you should build such a school. It would be a credit to you. But I think there are many tutors capable of running it for you and I do not feel I can accept the position."

"I shall have to bribe you further," he said, and drove them back to the Hall.

As the groom led away the grays, Sir Richard escorted Amelia into his home. A maid led her into a side chamber where she could remove her straw bonnet, comb back her hair, and wash away from her face and hands the dust of the morning ride. The maid cleaned Amelia's slippers with a cloth while Amelia puffed her short sleeves and fluffed out the skirt of her summer frock. It was a cream muslin printed with tiny sprigs of dark blue flowers, trimmed only with a neck ruffle of Clarisse's tatting and a long, blue-violet ribbon that matched Amelia's eyes. Of all her gowns it was the lightest, cut low in the bodice with sleeves that left her arms bare, and though she did not wholly like her own appearance in it, it was her most comfortable gown for such a warm day. Her objection to its style was that it made her look too young and perhaps a bit silly when she wished to look old and decorous.

When she joined Sir Richard in the dining hall, he said, "Miss Grant, may I present my son, Thomas?"

Amelia found herself looking down into a serious, eight-year-old version of Richard, complete with the thin face, thick brown-gold hair, light-brown eyes, and graceful, long-limbed form.

The child bowed politely, then came around behind her to hold her chair. When they were seated, the servants brought their midday meal of salmon and summer fruits and cheeses that Richard explained came from his estate. He discussed the health of his stock and his fields with Thomas, who answered seriously and with considerable knowledge. He was, Amelia thought, Richard without the laughter.

The rooms of the manor reflected generations of taste, being filled mostly with fine, beautifully cared-for pieces of furniture that spanned several styles yet were arranged together to complement each other.

There had been, she decided, no impetuous Wyland wives who threw away everything and ordered vast changes. Each had brought some treasure, some bit of her own taste, and added it. All, it would seem, had been women of discernment, no doubt women of high birth and extensive accomplishments.

Richard, who must have followed her glance, said, "It is rather a museum, I suppose. We Wylands seem unable to discard anything. My grandmother brought most of the porcelain from France. My mother collected many of the carpets when she traveled to India with my father. The furniture goes back three generations and is, I fear, a bit heavy."

"Oh, no," Amelia said, running her fingers over the cherrywood arms of her chair. "It is beautiful."

But what was most beautiful, she realized, was the Hall itself, for although its architecture was simple, even plain, its owners had apparently insisted that it catch the sun. Its windows were far wider than those in most manors, and glass-paned doors opened all the rooms to sunny garden courts, wide views, and grassy terraces.

"Then you will come to live with us and offer lessons for our tenants?" young Thomas asked. "That would be most kind of you, Miss Grant."

"I—I am not—I have not decided, Thomas."

"Please do decide in our favor," he said.

"I did not know you knew about your father's plans," Amelia said.

The boy looked surprised, then said seriously, "Rather, it was my thought, Miss Grant, that the tenants' children should be educated."

Richard said, "And an excellent suggestion, Thomas."

"I did need a bit of time to persuade him, but when Isabelle spoke of your school, I knew you could do such for us. And when I pointed this out, he quite saw the reason." The child returned his attention to his plate, leaving Amelia to gaze at Richard and wonder what his thinking truly was.

He did not attempt to explain further, but offered her muffins. She would have liked to ask, now that the subject had been brought up, where Isabelle was, yet she hesitated. When she did finally ask, later in the afternoon, she knew she had been right to delay the subject for a more private time.

After their meal Thomas excused himself and Richard insisted that Amelia rest awhile on the terrace. Annoyed, Amelia said, "Really, sir, I am not an invalid and I should not wish to be treated so. I was perhaps overtired at Aunt Sophie's home."

"You still look overtired to me," he said.

Amelia laughed, saying, "For a moment you looked almost as serious as Thomas. He is a sweet child, but does he never smile?"

"I will admit he is a bit of a puzzle to me. I do not think I was ever such a serious boy, though had I been, it would have pleased my parents." Tucking her hand in his arm, he strolled slowly toward the lake.

"You look so much alike."

"We do, I know, yet we are not alike. I truly do not understand the lad at all. We have little in common. I try to know him better, yet he is always so formal with me."

"He admires you."

"Do you think so? More often I fear I fall short of his expectations of me. He is as severe in his opinions as a parson, so that it sometimes occurs to me that he treats me more as his child than as his parent."

Amelia tried to keep her expression serious. "I am sure you well match his ideal of a father."

Richard rounded on her, swinging about so that Amelia realized with surprise that they had reached the lake and stood facing each other in the shadow of the overhanging willow. Sun glints filtered through its pale green leaves, sounds of lapping water echoed the afternoon calm, and the pungent fragrance of autumn leaves sweetened the air.

"Am I *your* ideal of a father?" he demanded.

"My—I—I do not understand."

"There is some reason why you wish to refuse to move to my home and supervise a school for me. It cannot be that you think you would be uncomfortable here. I can offer you far more luxury than the Puddleafton cottage. And you say you have no objection to teaching the servant children and I believe you. So it must be me of whom you do not approve."

Amelia's breath caught in her throat, making it quite impossible for her to speak.

"It is I," he said. "You do not wish to be near me. Or perhaps you fear my influence on Daphne. May I presume it has some connection with your own father, that you see in me the same weakness for gaming? Yet the circumstances are quite different, Miss Grant. I never hazard more than I can easily afford to lose."

When Amelia still could not reply, staring down at her slipper toes, her head bent forward in its straw-and-lace bonnet, he said, "Very well, Miss Grant, I cannot persuade you otherwise, but if you would hear out my plea, perhaps we could find an area of agreement that would give us both satisfaction. It seems clear to me that your objection to residing here is my own presence. Therefore, if you would come and organize the school, I would be gone when you were here, and I would give fair warning of my return so that you might then move back to Puddleafton during those short periods when I resided here."

Amelia stood in silence until she could do so no longer, then, without looking up, said, "You make me out a monster, willing to drive you from your home."

"It is I who must be a monster that you so dislike to be near me."

"I do not!" she cried, looking up, seeing the concern on his face, and then feeling hot tears press behind her eyelids. Catching up her skirt with her hand, she turned and ran away from him, unmindful of the direction or the sun's heat or her loss of dignity. The tears she had controlled so well until now chose this moment to escape and stream down her face, blinding her and running across her round cheeks. The gravel path tore at her thin slippers, the sun burned on her neck and arms, and her breath rose hot in her chest, nearly choking her.

The straw bonnet slid back and hung from its chin straps, the ribbons cutting at her throat, while her loosened hair tumbled about her face. When she could run no farther, Amelia stopped and leaned weakly against a tree trunk, her head buried in her arms.

She knew he stood beside her. She did not see or hear him but she could feel his presence. Yet there was nought to be done. Her dignity flung aside, she could not regain it, she could only lean weeping

240

against the tree, wishing she could somehow manage to swoon away. Then she would be carried to a couch somewhere and could pretend unconsciousness until she had quite controlled herself, letting him suppose her strange behavior to be no more than the result of a spell of summer fever.

Unfortunately, Amelia did not swoon easily and was too honest to pretend.

"Amelia," he whispered, so softly and so close that she fancied his lips must nearly touch her ear. "Amelia, what have I said?"

Her shoulders shook. She felt his hands gently close around her arms. He drew her away from the tree. She thought of kicking his ankle, she truly thought of it, knowing that what was happening should be prevented at once, but instead she turned in his grasp and let him settle her against his tall body, her head resting on his shoulder, her wet face buried in his silk waistcoat.

"Amelia, you cannot be this dismayed at my offer. There must be something else that offends you."

She sniffed loudly. With an arm still firmly about her, he pressed his handkerchief into her hands. She hid her face in the scent of freshly laundered, embroidered linen. Why was he forever rescuing herself and her sisters, catching them in swoons, pressing handkerchiefs and cups of tea into their shaking hands, soothing them with soft words? At times he behaved more like a nursemaid than a gentleman with the reputation of a rake. It was most unfair. Had he behaved like a rake, she would have known exactly how to treat him. True, she had little experience in handling rakes, but any gentlewoman knew well enough that such a male could be put and kept in place with aloof disdain.

Aloof disdain, Amelia knew, was difficult to manage while blowing one's nose. Worse, it was impossible to extend to a man who clucked sympathetically, held one gently, and stroked one's hair as though one were an unhappy child.

Yet her tears had barely ceased when he ceased treating her as a child. Indeed, he behaved very much as she had always thought a rake might well do, giving her the opportunity to regain her senses and apply disdain. Unfortunately, it required a few moments for Amelia to realize the change in their positions and collect her control, unused as she was to such behavior.

What caught her by surprise was his hand under her chin, tilting her tear-stained face to his. She looked into his warm eyes, saw a flicker of something that totally unnerved her, and then, though she should have guessed the meaning of that look, she was startled into stillness by the warmth of his mouth on her own.

Thought deserted her. She forgot who she was, where she was, and anything she might ever have known about disdain. The tingling problem that had disturbed her fingertips now raced through her whole body. Amelia clung to him, kissing him back.

Then, in a lightning flash that left her trembling, her wits returned. She pushed herself free of his arms.

"I cannot—you cannot—we cannot!" she sputtered.

To her horror he grinned and said, "Oh, I rather think we can."

"Sir Richard!"

"Could you not simply call me Richard? We are now well enough acquainted."

"You mock me!" Amelia turned to flee, but he caught her hand and would not release it.

"I do not mock you, Amelia," he said softly. "I love you."

She stopped trying to free herself, unable to think beyond his words. Her breath caught and for a moment she thought her heart had ceased its beating. But then it resumed, pounding so wildly that she feared he would hear it. Her face burned scarlet.

"Amelia, I had thought that if you were near me, staying in my home, you would one day learn to care for me. I must confess that as my reason for pursuing my son's suggestion of a school. But now I think I need no longer pretend with you. I think you already care at least a bit for me."

If Amelia had at one moment trembled with embarrassment, she now shook with fury. "Care for you! Truly, sir, you overstep the bounds! I will not be one of your flirtations! You dare not treat me so!"

"My flirtations? What flirtations?"

"I—I—" Amelia faltered. Did he expect her to name names? Did he think she would repeat village gossip? He knew quite well his own reputation. Surely he did not need her to explain it to him. She saw, to her dismay, that his face was innocent of deceit, his forehead lined with genuine concern.

When he said nothing, she continued, sputtering in her agitation, "Do not play your games with me, sir. Surely you cannot pretend that the marchioness was an elderly aunt or that you invited her here only because you had a guardian's interest in Lady Isabelle or—oh! And where *is* Isabelle? Where is the marchioness?"

"An elderly aunt!" he exclaimed, then chuckled. "She would not like that!"

"No doubt you have replaced her with another fine lady," Amelia snapped, then clasped her hands over her mouth. She had not meant to be so rude, yet he drove her to it.

In answer to her fury he gently smoothed back the stray curls that clung damply to her forehead. She jerked her head to escape his hand.

He said softly, "What a temper you have, my dear. I can see that if there is to be any relationship between us at all, I must forever be totally honest with you or you will presume the most outrageous conclusions."

"You owe me no explanations," Amelia cried, but her heart disclaimed this, praying he could explain to her satisfaction, yet not expecting that he could.

"Indeed, I do," he said. "For in truth, I used the marchioness badly in order to endear myself to you; yet I see my schemes went astray. I persuaded the marchioness to enroll her daughter with you so that I might have a ready excuse to see more of you, that is all."

"Oh, nonsense! She did not leave her home and reside with you simply to—oh! Why did you need an excuse to see me?"

"I am sure I cannot say. Had you been any other woman, Miss Amelia Grant, I should simply have knocked on your door, introduced myself, and said straight out my intentions. But I could not do that with you, dear heart, as you had already contrived to use me in your own scheme."

"No such thing!" Amelia objected.

"Indeed? Did you not think to marry me to Berdine or to Clarisse, whichever would have me, with no thought of my wishes?"

Horrified to hear him state so bluntly the hopes she had intended to realize through subtlety, Amelia's mind raced and she cried, "How you do distract one! No doubt you hope thus to avoid explaining the marchioness."

He spread his hands in a gesture of defeat. "Ah, the marchioness. Her husband owns splendid hunting and fishing rights. I visit him autumns. The marchioness, however, finds Scotland a bore and longs for the social delights of the London Season, which is why she came here and why I took her then to London. I helped her find a suitable home in London and she is there now, as is Lady Isabelle."

"Do you expect me to believe that she came only to have you aid her in finding a London house?"

Then he really did laugh, his handsome face a wreath of small lines, his eyes sun-bright. He reached out and drew Amelia back into his arms, saying, "You have a wicked mind, Amelia Grant, you truly do. You are not the pure innocent I once thought you. And as I have sworn to be honest with you, I will admit that the marchioness had in mind more from me than aid in finding a house. But as truthfully can I say that aid in her London search and the hospitality of my home are all that she received from me. She is not a type of woman whom I either admire or desire."

As she could not look into his face without causing

her heart to pound unreasonably, Amelia laid her head on his chest and abandoned herself to the momentary madness that flamed in her mind. It would pass, like a fever, and she would regain her composure as well as her common sense, she fervently hoped.

Pressing his face against hers, he asked, "Are you not going to ask what sort of woman I desire?"

"No," Amelia sniffed.

"Then I must tell you anyway. If you will not have me, Amelia, I shall be doomed to a life of bachelorhood and loneliness."

"What—what do you mean, *have* you?" she said into his waistcoat.

"What could I possibly mean? Do you think I should make an indecent offer to the niece of Sophie Stafford? Were you someone else, I might be tempted, love, but as you have as your guardian angels both Miss Stafford and my grandmother, two of the most terrifying beings I have ever encountered, I must keep my emotions under control and wait out a proper marriage offer, posting of banns, betrothal parties—Amelia, I do hope you realize how much I must love you to suffer through so much."

And suddenly Amelia did. She said slowly, "I do not know what to tell you, Richard. You are kind and dear and—and—"

He held her away from him, puzzled. "Do you not love me, then?"

"I—I—" Amelia looked everywhere but at him, though her hands still rested on his chest, her fingers twisting nervously at his waistcoat buttons.

"Was I wrong? Could I be so wrong?"

246

"No. No—I do love you, Richard—"

"Then say yes!"

"I cannot!" Amelia cried. "I cannot, Richard, you do not understand! Now, here, this moment, you make promises, and I know you mean them, but you have happily remained single these many years, you enjoy your freedom, you are the favorite of all hostesses, charming all the ladies, you—you frequent the gaming tables, you—I do not know what all, but I cannot think I could fit into such a life—"

"But you were willing that I should marry your sister!" His hands dropped from her shoulders and he stepped back, suddenly rigid. His fists clenched at his sides and his knuckles whitened. She saw the muscles in his jaw tighten.

She forced herself to answer, her voice shaking. "I—I would not have let you marry Clarisse. Berdine, I think—that is, I thought Berdine—she is so religious, you see—"

"You thought Berdine could save my soul?" he shouted.

"I—I suppose that's it," she whispered.

"You listen to me, Amelia Grant, it would take more than a few prayers to save me. It would take a very strong woman with spirit and temper and a quick, clever mind to even begin to—Amelia?"

Amelia bent her head into her hands. She stamped her foot in fury, this time at herself because she could not make the silly tears stop. She went right on sobbing while he held her, stroked her shoulders, brushed back her hair, kissed her forehead and cheeks and then her mouth.

"Abandon me if you will," he murmured, "but I shall lay the responsibility of my doomed soul on your doorstep."

"Oh, Richard," she giggled through her tears, "if that is so, then I think I must needs marry you and save you."

CHAPTER 19

Later Amelia admitted to Richard that he had been absolutely right, that she had forced on him an unforgivable amount of suffering. But how could she have known?

"I ask you," she said as they walked arm in arm along the gravel path, her fur-lined bonnet pulled forward to protect her face from the crisp air, "how could I have known? Berdine's wedding was such a simple ceremony."

"Berdine did not marry my grandmother's grandson," Richard said, and pressed his large, warm hand over her gloved fingers.

Snow drifted like blossom petals through the bare limbs of the oaks. Amelia smiled, remembering.

There had been parties, parties, parties, so that she might be presented to all of Richard's friends presumably, but those friends had turned out to be far past Richard's age, crowds of white-haired, bent gentlemen and ladies, rustling about her in clouds of powder and ruffled silk and glittering diamonds.

They had fussed and whispered, their whispers as loud as shouts as they leaned over each other's hearing horns.

"Pretty thing. Who is she? Miss Stafford, you say?

Didn't know there was a Miss Stafford that young. Oh! Miss Stafford's niece! Why didn't you say that at first? Doesn't look a bit like Sophie, does she? Quite a beauty, eh?"

Amelia had blushed and smiled and tried to hear only what she was meant to hear, while Richard, no help at all, stood at her side laughing and repeating the worst of the comments.

While she tried to look dignified, he whispered in her ear, "Good healthy filly, that one. Should add good blood to the Wyland line, eh, gel?"

At such moments she seriously considered not marrying him at all. However, as the banns had been posted and the parties given, she could not think of a way to withdraw.

Once she had hissed back at him, "Were it not that I dislike creating scandal, I should call off the whole marriage."

His answer had been to lead her firmly from the reception hall to an alcove beneath a staircase where he had kissed her until she confessed, "I did not mean it, Richard." Then, flushed and breathless, she had followed him back to the party, all too aware of the eyebrows raised in their direction.

During their moments alone she had scolded him, saying, "I cannot think how you expect me to impress all these people whom your grandmother wishes me to impress if you insist on whispering embarrassing words in my ear."

"If I must suffer, everyone must suffer," he said firmly.

"You are not suffering."

"What visible signs do you wish to see? Shall I

fling myself on the floor sobbing? Shall I gnash my teeth and rip at the draperies?"

"But why are you suffering?" Amelia demanded.

"Until after the wedding, dear heart, I am no more than an accessory, an escort, a piece of decoration to serve as background to the bride."

"You are no such thing! You are the groom!"

"Nonsense. No one cares a whit for the groom."

"But then I must needs feel guilty!"

He had laughed at that. "If guilt increases your feelings for me, I shall encourage it. Perhaps you would care to kiss me and soothe away my pain?"

"Oh, Richard, you are a wretch," she had said, but she had also kissed him.

Amelia's wedding day was golden with October sunlight. The oaks formed dark russet canopies and the asters spread rich purple carpets for the guests who filled the Wyland gardens. The still air shimmered, heavy with the fragrance of drying grass and late flowers. Richard, Amelia thought, was no accessory. Dressed in pale fawn satin, he held the enraptured gaze of every disappointed mother of an eligible. Thomas, in brown velvet, stood beside him.

Daphne and Clarisse had preceded Amelia to the flower-decked altar, their soft autumn-green silk gowns blending with the garden. Amelia had walked slowly from the house, trembling in her pale-blue silk so that its violet ribbons fluttered, her dark hair hidden beneath her blue silk bonnet, her chin held high above the violet bow that matched her eyes. The Wyland diamonds sparkled around her slender throat. At her side Mr. Edmond Chicore, splendidly turned out in matching green, trembled almost as

251

much as Amelia. She could feel his arm shaking beneath her hand.

Aunt Sophie had said that as Amelia's father could not return for the wedding, Amelia should be accompanied by Richard's grandfather, but though Amelia had met and immediately adored the old earl, she had been adamant on this one point. Mr. Chicore must escort her on her wedding day so that everyone could clearly see that Mr. Chicore, regardless of his profession or family connections or any other rumors, was a recognized member of the Wyland family and must so be considered.

Mr. Measure, also at Amelia's insistence over Aunt Sophie's preference for a higher church official, had been chosen to perform the rites. Berdine had declined to be part of the ceremony as she feared that she might feel faint. Instead she sat on a garden bench with Aunt Sophie, her face glowing with the memory of her own wedding day.

Beyond the brilliance of the garden and the assembled crowd, Amelia could remember nothing other than the moment she stood by Richard's side, her vision so blurred with terror that she had felt certain she would swoon away. Then Richard's hand had closed over hers. She had looked up past her bonnet rim.

A wicked smile then had turned up the corners of his mouth and one eyelid had dropped in a most improper wink. Amelia's fear had fled as she fought to hold back a giggle.

Months later, as they wandered together through that same garden, its trees now bare, its shrubberies glittering with ice, Amelia still recalled with amazement the ceremony and the banquet and the dancing that continued on and on throughout the night until the next day's sunrise finally brought an ending to what seemed to have been a month and a half of parties.

"I cannot think how we ever survived," she admitted to Richard.

"It is all for good purpose," he said.

"Is it? Why is that?"

"Ah, did you not know? All the confusion and turmoil and exhaustion of a wedding and its preparation are meant as a test of one's endurance, my love. Having withstood it all, we will find that the rest of our lives seem, by comparison, like a restful stroll through a garden."

Amelia slapped his arm affectionately, saying, "It is not a question of *seem,* Richard. That is exactly what our life *is.* Now, come along, the children will be expecting you to call them all by name and pat their heads. Did you remember the sweets for them?"

Richard felt in his pocket, then nodded. At the bottom of the garden where the new schoolhouse stood, Daphne and young Tom leaned out from the open doorway and waved frantically for them to hurry.

Richard complained, "With Tom and Daphne and you forever thinking up new projects for me and rushing me about, my garden strolls are becoming more like footraces."

Her face serious, Amelia said, "But Richard dear, you did tell me that you placed the responsibility for your soul's salvation on my doorstep."

Richard glared. The telltale dimple twinkled at the corner of Amelia's lower lip.

Ignoring Tom and Daphne, Richard stopped, drew Amelia into his arms, and, despite her mild protests, kissed her.

Love—the way you want it!

Candlelight Romances

Candlelight Ecstasy Romances

At your local bookstore or use this handy coupon for ordering: